CW00683840

The TERATOLOGIST

EDWARD LEE
WRATH JAMES WHITE

The
TERATOLOGIST

EDWARD LEE
WRATH JAMES WHITE

OVERLOOK CONNECTION PRESS
2007

TERATOLOGIST
© 2003 by Edward Lee and Wrath James White
Interview © 2007 Dave Hinchberger

Dust Jacket Illustration © 2007 by Alan M. Clark

Published by
Overlook Connection Press
PO Box 1934, Hiram, Georgia 30141
www.overlookconnection.com
overlookcn@aol.com

First Edition

Signed Limited Hardcover
ISBN 1-892950-82-0
A signed limited hard cover of 500 copies
is available from OCP and Specialty Bookstores.
You can view complete details at:
www.overlookconnection.com

Hard Cover
ISBN: 1-892950-85-5

This book is a work of fiction. All rights reserved. No part of this book may be reproduced or transmitted in any form or by any means, electronic or mechanical, without the written permission of the Publisher, The Overlook Connection Press.

Book Design & Typesetting:
David G. Barnett/Fat Cat Design

THE TERATOLOGIST

Sharon could see and hear and, to a degree, think. But she couldn't speak—she'd been born without vocal cords. She couldn't make a peep, and she guessed that was the chief reason why the men who worked here liked to come in and do things to her. She couldn't very well tell anybody—the home's director, for instance— that she was being routinely raped in a facility that existed to help people like her, yet on the other hand, she didn't really mind. It was sensation, nearly all she was likely to get, given her condition.

They left the TV on, toward which she would loll her head, drooling on the rank pillow, her visual universe limited to whatever channel they chose to leave on, typically Channel 9: soap operas and talk shows. Hence, her lot in this strange life, to lie in the raised bed, to be fed sweet mush by nurses (Sharon had no teeth), to watch Jerry Springer, and to go to sleep every night after being fastidiously copulated with.

Her missing vocal cords were just one sequent symptom of her hypo-osteopesis, a rare genetic affliction also less-than-clinically referred to as "curled-bone syndrome." Her I.Q. was about 70, that of a low-level retardate, because as an infant, defected cranial development prevented her brain from growing into the proper shape. Her head was warped. The rest of her affliction left all of her long bones curled up like bows of pasta, the ribs on her right side curled inward, the ribs on her left curled out, and her hips splayed like a book lying open flat. *Why don't they just kill her?* one of the janitors had muttered under his breath one time when he was in here changing her pan. *Ain't gonna get better— that mess? Just suckin' up tax dollars... Yeah, someone oughta just kill her.* Sharon wasn't sure but she thought she knew what *kill* meant, and she didn't want that, not really. She thought about what it might be like, but if they killed her then she supposed she would no longer be able to watch Springer, and she liked Springer. Sometimes they had people akin to her on the show, and she enjoyed seeing them, a relativity, perhaps. She especially liked the one with the girl with no arms and legs, who walked about on her buttocks. A man had even married her! Hope, perhaps, in view of the cruel joke nature had played on her.

No men would be likely to marry Sharon, though. They'd just come in here and fuck her every night, unmindful of her wafting pissy odors and staggering halitosis.

At ten o'clock, the night nurse turned off the TV and lights. She pulled the covers up, sniffing. "Wasn't Louie supposed to give you your weekly sponge bath today?" the woman asked, knowing that Sharon couldn't answer. "Lord, you don't smell very good, honey. Not my problem, though." She left in the dark. Sharon knew the routine now. About a half hour later, the door clicked back open and Louie entered. It was his job to check each patient several times throughout the night, to see if they'd died; most of the people in the state home were old—that's what Sharon had heard. In fact, she was the youngest patient on the wing, twenty-five. Every now and then doctors from research centers and medical schools would come by to examine her. And always comment to each other how remarkable it was that she'd survived this long. Sometimes Louie would comment too, whispering to her as he lay between her curled legs, "I hope you don't die for a long time, sweetie. I hope to be squirting my load in you for years to come!"

Louie only turned on the little light with the bendable arm over the med chart, to keep it dark, but Sharon could still see him plainly. Tall and skinny, with stooped shoulders. Bald in the middle, with wiry gray-black hair sticking out on the sides. Pits in his face looked like someone had cleated him. "Lovin' time, sweetie," the familiar whisper announced. "Lovin' time." "Jesus, she stinks!" another male voice whispered back. Sometimes Louie brought other men here too. "Yeah, that's great, ain't it, Phil?" Louie replied. "I love the stinkers. I'm supposed to wash her but I can usually get away only doing it once a month." "Good Christ!"

She heard them cluttering, could see them moving about. Sharon had never seen the other man before, a fat guy with a doughy face.

"And you—you—you're...going to *fuck* her? Smelling like that?"

"Yeah. I love it. Take a look." Louie bent the little light around, shined it on Sharon and pulled her gown up. "Ain't that sweet, Phil?"

Phil's fat face bloomed, cheeks billowing. He croaked, "Good Lord," and then jerked away. Sharon knew by the wet, splattering sound that he was vomiting in the trashcan.

Louie chuckled. He blew his nose into his hand and rubbed the mucus over Sharon's gaping vagina. Then he climbed on. "God, you smell like shit," he grunted, humping her immediately. "It just—turns me—the fuck-*on!*"

Phil had finished relocating the contents of his stomach into the garbage. He stood back up against the wall in the dark. "You are one sick motherfucker."

"Yuh—yeah!"

"How can you even get it up? The smell alone'll kill my sex drive for a year."

"Naw, man. Try it once, you'll never be the same."

"At least fuck her in the ass. You get her pregnant, there'll be big trouble."

"Shit, Phil. She's a genetic monster. Her genes are so fucked up she couldn't get knocked up in a million years." Louie just kept humping while Sharon's motionless limbs joggled on the bed. Her breasts joggled too, like baggies of vanilla pudding, depending into her hairy armpits. "No fetus could ever live in his fucked up womb."

"Yeah? *She* lived."

Louie wasn't concerned. "Ah—ah—ah, you shitty *bitch!* Ahhh!"

Sharon could feel the warm trickle go into her as his thrusts slowed, then stopped. "Aw, fuck. What a nut..." Eventually he rolled off, heaving in breath.

"And how often do you do this?" Phil asked, astounded in his revulsion.

"Couple times a night. Couple other guys on the floor do too."

Phil's face seemed pinched up in the dark. "You're all a bunch of scat freaks. I've never seen anything so sick in my life."

Louie chuckled. "Hey, wanna make a bet?"

"What bet?"

Louie bent the light around some more, shined it right between Sharon's sweaty legs. "Bet ya fifty bucks you ain't got a set brass enough to eat that pussy."

Phil teetered in place, as though simply hearing the words might cause him to pass out. "I'd *kill* myself before I'd do that."

"Amateur!" Louie looked like the demented scatological erotopath he was, standing there in his white work tunic and no pants. He extended his hand toward Sharon's pale and malodorous form. "Sure you don't want to take a bang? It's good pussy, man."

Phil put a paw to his bulbous gut. The answer was invariably no.

"Suit yourself. I got more work to do."

The other man could barely remain standing in his dismay. "Let's get out of here before we get caught! You had your fun, let's go. You're telling me you aren't done yet?"

The big toothy grin seemed to glow in the dark. "I ain't even *close* to being done, brother. You wanna see hardcore? *I'll* show you hardcore—"

Phil's stomach was making fish-tank noises in objection. "No no no, please, God no," he pleaded as Louie—shit-splotched balls swinging—climbed back up on the bed, on his knees. He was poised like a child about to push a peanut with his nose. "Oh, yeah, baby," he chuckled. He parted Sharon's bowed legs wide. "This is better than desert—"

"No, no, no, please, God no—"

"—Yeah, man, like a big cream pie—"

And then Louie, with no hesitation nor compunction, proceeded to execute the act of cunnilingus on a drooling, insensate Sharon. "La la la la la," he burbled. The noise of the act sounded like a big ravenous dog devouring a pile of Alpo.

"How can you do that? She's been shitting and pissing in a bed pan all day!"

"La la la la la—"

Louie's tongue delved deep. At one point it looked like he was trying to push his entire face into the slack, nauseating mass of her vagina. Then came the obvious slurping sounds, which made Phil, quite gruelingly, think of someone sucking up the last of a milkshake through a McDonald's straw. But there was no milkshake down in that furrow of filth. Louie was reclaiming his own semen, quite greedily.

Phil fell back to his knees, to vomit some more in the trash. The regurgitation sounded like a drain backing up. When there was nothing left, he stayed down there a while, dry heaving as strings of bile dangled off his lips.

"What a light-weight," Louie chuckled, smacking. "It's like eating chocolate cake."

He looked up from the parted thighs, runny excrement, semen, and pubic hairs around his mouth. "And you wanna know the best part? I'm on the clock! I'm eating this shit-bag's cunt and getting paid eight bucks an hour!"

The image alone, evidently, kept Phil where he was, and this was a good thing. He didn't need to see what Louie was doing now: sucking Sharon's toes, dirty inch-long yellow nails and all. His penis stiffened in no time—long and thin, like the rest of him. The glands looked like a pair of arthritic knuckles, with a glimmering hole in the middle. He rearranged himself on the bed, parted his ass-crack and carefully placed it over Sharon's agape mouth. Then he began to vigorously masturbate. His stomach muscles tightened and loosened, tightened and loosened, along with periodic grunts, and then he whispered, "Phil, Phil! Watch this, it's really cool! I'm gonna shit in her mouth same time as I come." His hand shucked and shucked; he grunted some more. "She'll eat it, too—she's so stupid she thinks it's food!"

In actuality, Sharon did not think it was food but she essentially had no choice but to consume what he expelled into her mouth—otherwise she'd gag. Even if she had any significant mobility, her mind was too undeveloped to understand defensive impulses, such as biting, but she couldn't bite him anyway because she had no teeth. She simply lay there, quivering as her air supply was depreciated. At one point her coated tongue wagged upward and accidentally licked Louie's distended anus, which was just beginning to dilate. His loathsome scrotum slapped her crooked chin...

Then—

Snap!

Clink!

The great weight on Sharon's face was suddenly gone. Had Louie fallen off in his fervor? He'd disappeared over the side of the bed and didn't get back up again. Sharon wasn't capable of wondering much about it, but she instinctively sucked in fresh breaths of air now that her nose and mouth were no longer obstructed.

Did she see a shadow roving to one side of her?

Phil had stood back up, wiping his mouth. "Louie? Where'd you go?

Snap!

Clink!

Phil toppled to the floor. He was gone, too.

The nicest voice Sharon had ever heard beckoned her. Though she wouldn't have known the distinction, the words rolled out in a soft, articulate British accent. The voice said this:

"Hi, there. You must be Sharon. I stopped those bad men from doing what they were doing. I'd like to take you out of this place, to a much better place where you'll be washed and cared for and you'll get to eat good food. Would you like that, Sharon? Would you like to go someplace nicer than here?"

Sharon, of course, couldn't answer, but she quivered where she lay in response to the question. *Yes yes yes!* she thought. More than anything else in the world, she'd like to go to a place nicer than this.

"Here. Let me help. I'll take you out of here right now."

Hands were on her, strong arms sliding under her back and her thighs. She was being lifted up and then she was very gently placed in a wheelchair.

"We're on our way. You'll like where I'm taking you, I promise."

She rolled through darkness. The door clicked open and then she was being wheeled out into the hall outside. Sharon rarely saw this hall. It was bright and very quiet. Her warped head lolled to one side, a string of drool trailing. It was fun being pushed along. Every so often, though, something passed in her field of vision: people. A nurse, then a doctor, then an intern. A janitor, another nurse, a security guard. They were all lying sprawled on the floor, unmoving. Behind each of their heads, a halo of blood bloomed, shiny like wet paint.

Sharon was too excited and confused and simply too mentally deficient to deduce what had happened to them all: they'd all been shot dead, each by a single small-caliber bullet to the head.

"I've a nice big comfy van waiting to pick us up outside, Sharon," she could hear the British man saying behind her. "It's even got a television in it. We'll watch anything you like. Would you like that?"

Oh yes yes yes yes! Sharon's misfiring brain thought.

The wheelchair stopped. She heard a door open in front of her. Her head drooped—she had almost no control of her neck muscles so she couldn't incline her head. What was happening? Another voice, not the British man's:

"Hey! You!"

Sharon couldn't move her neck but she could move her eyes, and she strained them forward and to the right. At the end of the hall stood one of the home's security guards.

"Visiting hours were over at—" The guard's objection ceased when he noticed all the bodies lying in the hall.

"I'm not here to visit, friend," the British voice sprang out behind her. "I'm abducting this critical-care patient. And, yes, I'm obviously the one who killed all the staff on this floor."

The nice man's hand shot up, gripping something. Sharon could only piece the generalizations together by what she'd seen on TV. No way, of course, for her to know precisely what the British man held in his hand: a Walther PPKs with an M9-SD integral quick-detach 40db sound suppressor. Then came a:

Snap!

—As the diminutive weapon's slide cycled, and then a:

Clink!

—As one expended .380 brass cartridge arced out of the ejection port and hit the floor. There was no other sound. The sub-sonic hollow point hit the security guard in the bridge of the nose and he fell down like a hinged duck. A circle of blood spread behind his head on the glistening tile floor.

"There. We're off now, Sharon."

The British man wheeled her off the floor and out into the warm, windy night where a coal-black van sat in wait.

(I)

Westmore lit a generic cigarette and sputtered. The flight from LAX to Metro Detroit International had been delayed an hour on the runway because the ventilation system wasn't working. "Can't I just get off the plane for a few minutes and smoke while you're fixing the motherfucker?" he asked the stew. He was told he could not, but, if he liked, he could get a different flight with another airline. Then there was the fat guy sitting next to him who smelled like he hadn't washed his shirt in a year. *It's my karma,* Westmore resigned. Now he was sitting in the airport bar waiting for what's-his-name-Bryant, the journalist. Westmore typically drank beer but after the grueling flight, he wanted to start with a little kick. He ordered a scotch and water and gasped at the first sip.

"Do I look like I'm in the Rat Pack?" he griped to the barmaid. "I ordered a scotch and water. This seems to be sufficiently lacking the water."

She smirked back, too much lipstick, and bad hair. The blond perm looked like a pile of curly fries on her head. "Most drunks don't complain when you pour them a hard drink."

Westmore, actually, appreciated the snide answer. He believed that what didn't kill him made him stronger. "You got me pegged that fast?"

"It's easy, buddy. Most drunks are bad tippers, too."

"I like you already! Are you married?"

She wandered away to some other chores, while Westmore nursed the scotch. It must be a rail brand, tasted like kerosene. When he looked around, he noticed he was the only one in the bar, and beyond, the airport concourse looked almost empty.

It was only eleven a.m., which didn't help Westmore's impressions. It was the dichotomy: the safety of the late-morning and the black cloud he felt hovering over his head. He knew he wasn't psychic but whenever he got the willies before a shoot, something often rang true. Like when he'd gone to the Hamptons to interview the famous abstract painter in the fussy beach house. Westmore thought his art looked like someone tossing paint on a canvas, not too tough a trick. The old geezer had croaked in his armchair before Westmore even had time to get a light reading. Heart attack. *What am I supposed to do!* he screamed to the fates. *Take pictures of a fuckin' corpse?* Then there was the time the magazine had flown him to Redmond, Washington, to shoot some pictures of Bill Gates. Westmore got some serious willies on the way to the airport. His cab got a flat in rush hour on Sepulveda and he'd missed his flight. The plane crashed.

He had some big time willies right now.

Then he thought one word, one name. Farringworth.

Even the name sounded pinky-in-the-air, like Carnegie, Van Buren, and Rothschild. *Thirty-year-old multi-billionaire,* Westmore thought. It was nothing new to him; he'd been snapping pix of these caviar-scarfing snobs five years. Bluebloods. Their fucking handkerchiefs cost more than Westmore's best suit. But what the hell was putting the butterflies in his gut? Bryant would know more.

They worked for *Blue Chip* magazine, a Forbes clone that had taken off. He'd teamed with Bryant on a couple jobs in the past—Trump, Rockefeller's kid, and some Indian Chief who owned the biggest casino in the country, in Connecticut of all places. Best thing about Bryant was he didn't fuck around. Westmore'd snap the pix right off, and Bryant would take his notes, and they were out of there. He hoped this gig would go as well.

He glanced around, bothered. He didn't like being the only person in a bar; it made him feel like a man with a problem, which he supposed he had. "Hey, how come nobody's in the bar?"

"Because you're here?" she answered.

"Beautiful *and* witty."

"Hate to tell you this, killer. Not many people drink this early."

"Ah, there is that…"

She meandered away just as a massive shadow crossed Westmore's back.

"Isn't it a little early to be drinking?"

Westmore frowned. "Everybody seems to be telling

me that today." Bryant stepped up to the bar: black, shaved head, six-five, two-fifty, and zero body fat. The barmaid winked at him. *Figures,* Westmore thought.

Bryant didn't look like a writer. He looked like a kick-boxer or something, he looked like the kind of guy who could clear out a shit-pit bar full of rednecks with one arm. He wore a suit and tie, while Westmore wore jeans, Velcro sneakers, and a t-shirt that read CAPTAIN KIDD'S SEAFOOD MARKET, REDONDO BEACH.

"We're interviewing a billionaire today," Bryant reminded him. "Did you have to get so dressed up?"

"Come on, these Velcro sneakers cost ten bucks. At K-Mart." Then Westmore raised his overly stiff drink. His hand was shaking.

"What's wrong with you?" Bryant asked next. "Even *I've* never seen you this jittery so early in the day."

What could Westmore say? "I've just...got a bad vibe, you know?"

"No, I don't know."

"Something's giving me the willies about this one."

"Who? Farringworth? He's just another billionaire. We see these guys all the time. They're like sports stars, they're all the same and they're all assholes."

"The guy's thirty years old," Westmore pointed out. "How'd he get to be a billionaire by thirty?"

"Spot trading on the 4X. On a average there's about three trillion dollars a day trading. Farrington's an institutional trader whose clients have to put up a minimum of ten million dollars per transaction. He gauges global monetary fluctuations on a minute-to-minute basis. Farrington watches everything as it happens, from New York to Tokyo, Switzerland to Hong Kong, from Dollar to Yen to Deutschmark to Guilder to Lire to Ruble. His own profits he juggles through authority loan markets, interbank markets, yearling bonds, sterling money contracts, and flexible competitive-range ventures."

Westmore's face scrunched up. "Well, I guess whatever just came out of your mouth answered my question."

"What are you worried about? We know he's legit. IRS and SEC audit the guy out the ass every year. What, you think he's secretly funneling biological weapons to Iraq? He a front for white-slavers? That's what you thought about the last guy."

"I don't know what it is. I just feel weird."

"Westmore. You *are* weird. Rejoice in who you are."

"Boy, for a guy who complained about his drink being too stiff, you sure downed that in a hurry," the barmaid observed of Westmore's empty glass.

"May I have a Corona Light, this time, please?" Westmore asked. The bad scotch scorched his stomach.

"Isn't that also the name for the end of a penis?" she brought to mind, then put an opened bottle in front of him.

"That's on the house, right?" Westmore asked.

"No but it can be on your head if you like."

Bryant ordered an orange juice; when she gave it to him she said, "Now *that's* on the house."

"It's my karma," Westmore excused. "But I don't care. I'm a Kierkegaardian existentialist." This was what Westmore always said because it was easier and less humiliating that saying *I'm a fuckin' social failure and it doesn't bother me any more.* "So, what? Farringworth's meeting us here?"

"His people are picking us up and taking us to his house in Bloomfield Hills. It's the highest per-capita-income community in the world. Iacocca lives there,

John Ford, Trump's got a house, plus any CEO of any car manufacturer."

"What else you know about Farringworth?"

"He did his undergrad at Cornell, then got his MBA in international finance at the Wharton School, started at Fidelity as an investment analyst, studied under Peter Lynch. Rose through the ranks, got promoted to fund manager. They make a couple million a year. Everything after that was his own creativity. Took him five years in the field, and then—"

"Then he's a billionaire."

"I agree, it's a little unusual for a guy to get that rich that quick." Bryant shrugged. "But it happens."

"I guess some guys are just lucky," Westmore said.

"But not you, I'll bet," the barmaid chimed in. "I'll bet you *never* get lucky."

"I got lucky today, didn't I? I met you."

The barmaid rubbed the corner of her eye, with her middle finger.

"You're right," Bryant agreed. "It's your karma."

Westmore didn't argue. "All right, there's some historical info available about the guy, we know how old he is—oh, and I heard he wasn't married."

"Nope, never been. No kids, no rumors about girlfriends, stuff like that. A year ago there was an unauthorized biography. The hack who wrote it claimed he interviewed lots of people who went to school with Farringworth, and they all said they never saw him with a girl."

"Maybe he's a balls-across-the-nose kind'a guy," Westmore eloquently suggested.

"No, because no one ever saw him with a guy, either."

"If I had Farringworth's loot I'd have every girl in the Atlanta Cheetah Club living with me, but this guy's never even been *seen* with a chick?"

"Odd. The guy who wrote the bio said he dug back further but found nothing about his family background, either. And there aren't any photographs of him. College graduation pic says photo not available."

This perked Westmore up. "So I'll be the first—"

"The first guy to officially take his picture for any public forum."

"What about the book? Weren't there any pictures of him in that?"

"Nope."

"Shit, I didn't even there *was* a book about the guy."

"Well, there wasn't, really. This is just stuff that the author told me, some old putz down in St. Pete."

Westmore was confused, a fairly familiar condition. "Fill me in. There was a book or there wasn't?"

"This guy wrote one, got a contract for it but when Farringworth heard about it, he paid the publisher ten times their projected net profits to *not* publish it. At least that's what the writer said."

"Farrington sounds like some kind of gunned-up Howard Hughs, recluse to the max. Then all of a sudden he agrees to be interviewed for our magazine?"

"Change of heart, who knows," Bryant said, "or cares?"

"Yeah, and—Christ." Westmore looked up dreamily. "I'll be the first to get a picture of him. Why me?"

"Maybe it's your karma," Bryant alluded. "And as for the details, I guess we just sit here and wait till his people pick us up."

Westmore looked at his K-Mart watch. "I can't wait

too long. I want to get this done quick. My flight out is at eleven, and I want my bad-karma ass right back in this bar by seven-oh-five."

"Seven-oh-*five?*" Bryant questioned.

"The Yankees play Boston tonight. Come on, man, get with it. The *Yankees,* the *Yankees.*"

"Yeah, but look what's playing now."

On the TV in the corner, a CNN newswoman was reciting the day's lead story: "—when pictures of Father Thomas Corelli arrived in the mailboxes of every registered member of St. Simon's Church. Corelli was a well-regarded pastor at the largest Catholic Church in Texas when he took a leave of absence early last month, according to diocesan authorities. However, police authorities say that the pictures depict Father Corelli engaged in various sex acts, though they wouldn't comment further, nor would the Diocese..."

"Looks like the Cat-Licks are taking on the chin again," Westmore said.

Bryant added: "Not just the Catholics. Last week there was that report of sex videos being delivered to a local TV station in Tennessee. The videos showed a guy sodomizing a collie, and the guy was a big wheel minister for the Baptist Church."

Westmore gaped. "You're shitting me."

"No, don't you watch the news? There've been several things like that going on the past few months. Another one in South Carolina, too, some Evangelist guy. Mpegs showed up on the internet. Same deal with all of them, they'd all either gone on vacation, or had a leave of absence. Organized religion is going to hell in a hand basket and fast."

It's a fucked up world, Westmore thought.

The next news-clip announced that the U.S. Air Force had dropped an 18,000-pound "daisy-cutter" bomb by mistake on a UN food storage facility in Afghanistan.

Yeah. Really fucked up...

"Mr. Bryant, Mr. Westmore." The voice was crisp, enunciated, and it took them by surprise. "I trust you haven't been waiting long?"

The pair turned quickly. Westmore stood up.

"I'm Philip Michaels, Mr. Farringworth's personal adjutant." Slim, short dark hair, sharp dark suit. "If you'll be so kind as to follow me, I'll take you gentlemen up to the house." Westmore fumbled for his camera bag, was about to leave, when the barmaid reminded, "Hey, dad, that'll be ten-fifty for the drinks."

Ho! At least kiss me first, honey! Remind me not to drink in airports... Westmore hurriedly paid, left her a buck tip, was about to pull off again, but then she said, "Don't forget your receipt. For your taxes. Never give Uncle Sam a break is what I say."

Yeah, yeah— He took the receipt and half-trotted out of the bar. When he went to stuff the slip of paper in his pocket he noticed that the barmaid had written her phone number on the back of it. *Well how do you like that?*

Maybe his karma was improving.

He caught up to Bryant and Michaels as they were exiting the doors at the baggage. The writer and "adjutant" were conversing casually. Westmore couldn't hear what they were saying, but he paused to wonder a possibility: *Maybe Farringworth's from England,* because his assistant, Michaels, had one hell of an obvious British accent. He leaned in closer to hear what Michaels and his partner were talking about.

"So what's Farringworth like anyway? What's it like working for the guy?"

"Those questions, unfortunately, I cannot answer. You will have to see for yourself."

"Are you serious?" Bryant asked, with his eyebrows raised suspiciously.

"Quite. I am under contract."

"So you can't tell me anything?"

"Well, I can tell you that if you are interviewing him in the hopes of finding some new business strategies you are wasting your time. Farringworth is somewhat of a savant."

"You don't just make over 300 million in your first year of trading, double that the second year and every year thereafter, without a solid grasp of the global market."

"Uh huh. Well, don't say I didn't warn you. Mr. Farrington's trading methods are mostly instinctual. He's like a good tennis player. He has a feel for where the ball is and where it's going to be the minute it's served and he only has to get himself into the right position to benefit."

"Yeah, it may sound simple but we're talking about multiple millions of dollars maneuvered through a constantly fluctuating global economic structure. It's not as simple as eenie meenie minie moe."

"Well, it would seem that for Mr. Farrington it is that simple."

"Hold on! Hold on one second!" Westmore spoke up, "Are you saying that we're not going to get anything from this guy? You mean we came all the way out here to get an interview so boring and unenlightening that the minute we get back to the office our editor will just toss the whole thing into the trash?"

"You may not get the interview that you were hoping for, but I assure you that it will be neither boring nor unenlightening." Michaels replied and the way he grinned made Westmore's skin suddenly feel as if it was too loose on him and a draft had slipped beneath it. They rode the rest of the way to the estate in silence. Michaels never stopped grinning.

(II)

Farringworth rose from the pool and stood naked on the marble tiles watching the droplets of water cascade over his thin, athletic physique, yet another thing that he barely had to work at. He had the metabolism of a teenager. Each drop of the heavily chlorinated water traced the outline of his perfectly defined musculature as it raced toward the floor. He flexed and the venous striated muscles became more pronounced like the "Anatomical Man" charts of the human muskuloskeletal that hung in hospital exam rooms.

John Farringworth was beautiful and he knew it. He was a flawless example of God's perfection, but he knew that creation was far from perfect. Betty smiled at him. Her dazzling diamond blue eyes sparkling out of a tragically pretty face attached to a monstrously malcrafted body. He watched the obese legless, armless thing glide through the water and he knew that God made mistakes. Betty was Farringworth's physical antithesis. A perfect example of God's creativity gone awry.

Unlike many severely deformed people who had been left to rot in hospitals with so little mental stimulation that their brains had turned to oatmeal, Betty was a near genius. She was Farringworth's secret weapon in the world of economy. A vast Intellect encased in a near useless overstuffed sack of flesh.

The young billionaire sat down by the edge of the pool and watched as the morbidly deformed "Walrus woman" that he'd rescued from a Russian freak show, undulated her girth through the water towards him. She had never been allowed much exercise in the circus save for her walrus tricks, balancing balls on her nose, catching fish in her mouth, and blowing horns. When his people discovered her, her circus handlers had her displayed in a shallow pool that Betty seldom entered for fear of drowning. Her inactivity had led to an excess of adipose tissue that put her weight well over 350lbs. Without arms or legs the extra fat gave her the appearance of giant water balloon.

Betty had been born with no limbs of any kind but rather one long aquiline torso ending in two stumps that had been intended to be thighs but had rather merged together into something that looked more like a tail. Wedged between them her sex was barely accessible. Farrington knew. He had tried to gain access to it on more than one occasion. Now he contented himself with the phenomenal blowjobs she could perform. Since he'd taught her to swim she'd not only lost quite a bit of weight but she'd also learned to hold her breath for a miraculously long time and since he'd started raping her esophagus with his cock, she'd completely lost her gag reflex. She could now deep throat like nobody's business.

Her gigantic breasts and mountainous ass were his two other favorite pleasure points. Betty had so many ripples and folds that just about any spot on her body could adequately substitute for pussy when properly lubricated. She was happy to pleasure him, to show her gratitude for the love and care that he gave her, and John took his fill, attacking her throat and ass on an almost daily basis, except when he was saving his strength for the angels. He loved to watch as she sucked down his seed with childlike enthusiasm, his erection throbbing in her throat, her lips buried in his pubic hair, and her eyes looking up into his for approval. He loved it when she smiled up at him after he'd bathed her face in semen and it dribbled off her lips and eyelids and even the tip of her nose. She never looked happier.

When John Farringworth's assistant had brought her here she could not move on her own power at all except to lift her head. She was so enclustered with fat that she was little more than a formless corpulent blob scarcely recognizable as human. Her skeleton was smothered beneath hundreds of pounds of useless tissue. She was a tragedy that utterly delighted Farrington. This was clearly an example of something that was not meant to be; an obvious mistake. "And on the 9th day God created Betty and said: 'Ooops!'"

Her body, which was now rather sausage shaped, looked then like that of a bloated leech engorged with blood. Her tremendous breasts had been nearly squashed flat and were blistered and calloused from lying on them. They had showed her how much lighter she was in the pool and had taught her to swim. The first day she was able to propel herself through the pool on her own power she had squealed with delight. That same night John seduced/molested her for the first time and she'd been more than willing to show her appreciation. Now she practically lived in the pool, waiting for John to come swim with her each day so that she could pleasure him. But today he didn't seem interested.

Betty glided to the edge of the pool where Farringworth sat with his limp penis dangling just above the water. She eased up beneath him and kissed and licked at his flaccid sex organ but Farringworth pushed her away.

"What's the matter John? Don't— don't you want me?" Anyone else looking at the beautiful billionaire and the twisted freak floating between his thighs would have thought her question absurd, but Betty knew that Farringworth adored her for some incalculable reason and his apathy now could only mean one thing... he was dreaming of angels.

"Nothing's wrong, my lovely. I'm just not in the mood right now." He was staring off across the pool with a sad forlorn expression marring his perfectly sculpted face. He didn't even look at Betty when he spoke.

"No, John. Don't. Please don't, John. Don't go in there again. They always hurt you. Just let me take care of you. I'll do anything you want. The angels are evil! They'll kill you!"

"Perhaps I like to be hurt, Betty. Perhaps I deserve it."

Farringworth stood up and dried himself off with one of the huge monogrammed beach towels that lay stacked on a rack by the pool house door.

"Don't go, John! I'll let you do anything you want! You can piss on me again if you want!"

John left the pool house, slamming the door in disgust. He was still nude as he strode down the hallway toward his harem. He reached the end of the hall where a wrought iron gate covered a huge wooden door. Both were locked and only Farringworth and his manservant Micheals possessed the key. The door separated one entire half of the house from the other half. Beyond that door an entire world lay separated from the rest of reality. Here horror, legend, and tragedy lived naked and resplendent. The beauty of nature in grotesque ruin displayed on silk sheets and satin pillows and clothed voluptuously in lace, leather, and latex. Wanton and irresponsible genetic failures limping, crawling, and slithering in appalling ill-crafted forms and near absences of form collected here by Farrington to shame God himself with his lack of perfection. Only Farrington was truly perfect and in his mind that entitled him to the seat now held by the lord of creation.

There were thirteen bedrooms on this side of the house. Ten of the bedrooms were occupied by one or more of Farrington's "lovers." The other three awaited new acquisitions. Some rooms he visited fairly regularly and others were reserved for his rarest moods, when only the most grotesque and revolting acts would soothe his desires.

John passed the room where his "Monster" lived and stopped to listen at the door. Inside he could hear squeals and screams, begging, crying, and praying followed by the guttural moans and grunts of his Monster. "Please! More!" a woman's voice pleaded. "God in Heaven-more!" John slipped his key into the lock and cracked the door.

The Monster was on the bed facing John. His name was Billy Meyers and he had one of the most horrible congenital disorders, the most severe case of

Neurofibromotosis anyone had ever seen. His skull had tremendous horn-shaped bone growths and massive tumors that stuck out as much as ten inches from the top of his head like gun turrets. His entire skull was elongated into something that looked like a watermelon. His overgrown jaw hung down to his chest and was filled with two extra rows of teeth on the bottom and one extra row on top. His face looked absolutely prehistoric with cheekbones that jutted out so far they looked like some type of armament. From that twisted lump of meat and bone shone eyes that gleamed with a madness so intense and ferocious that it was like staring into a burning sun. One eye was blue and the other was green yet Billy himself was black as obsidian. But it was his body where nature had been its cruelest. His chest and stomach were untouched and gave a hint of what he may have been. Finely sculpted, heavily muscled pecs like a weightlifter and a washboard stomach made up his torso yet suspended from them were arms so massive and twisted they looked barely functional. The tumors in his right arm were so pronounced that it looked like a kindergartener's drawing of a superhero with misplaced muscles that were little more than lumps and bulges. His left arm was longer than the right and was just one thick tube with no visible elbow. His hips were tilted askew and massive legs like the gnarled trunks of some malformed tree erupted from them. Billy Meyers made the elephant man look like James Dean.

This mistake had spent most of his life in hospitals and state foster homes. His parents had left him in the hospital soon after he was born and had never returned to reclaim him. He'd been alone and unloved his entire life until he'd come to the mansion. It was his eighteenth birthday when Farringworth arrived at the juvenile correction facility where Billy was being held on aggravated sexual assault charges. After Billy hit puberty and realized that no one would want to have sex with someone so freakish of their own freewill he'd begun breaking into the homes of elderly women and raping them in their beds. No one knew how many he had done before he'd been caught. He'd been incarcerated for three years before Farringworth had come to claim the young monster for his collection.

Bent over in front of Billy was a middle-aged nun chained at the wrist and ankles and squeezed into a latex bustierre that pushed her fat oversized breasts up around her neck. She had a choke collar around her neck with the leash firmly gripped between Billy's countless teeth. Her face was turning blue as she struggled to scream, but even though that blue tint, there was a wantonness raging. From the waist down she was naked... and bleeding. Billy was ramming a fireplug shaped penis roughly eight inches long and nearly seven inches around with a head the size of an apple into her puckered anus as she shrieked and begged and cried out for her savior. Farrington could only hope that he would hear her and come.

The Metopronil's working better than anyone could imagine, John thought. Who could argue? He'd dumped a hundred million dollars of his own pocket change under the table into Daye Pharmaceuticals' coffers so they'd continue developing the new sexual stimulant that FDA had banned further research on. Metopronil, ideally, was to be the next generation of Viagra-like drugs, not only stimulating blood flow to the groin but stimulating libidinal hormone activity. In the end, the technicians at Daye grimly realized that the little red pill worked too well, turning even the most sexually uninspired into rapists and unslakable erotopaths. "What you want me to do is illegal!" the president of Daye had insisted to John. "It's a federal offense. We can't develop this stuff anymore." "Develop it exclusively for me," John had replied and left the office of company's Grotten, Connecticut, headquarters. That's when Michaels had started bringing in the suitcases full of untraceable cash. Money talked.

The appearance was crucial. *There must be lust in their eyes, there must be true desire.* Otherwise the videos, pictures, and internet feeds would be seen for what they actually were: forced performances. It was one thing to force nuns and priests into sexual scenarios, but it was another to make them willing. The drug made them willing. There were no guns to their heads here, and the videos would easily pick that up. What the public would see were celibate servants of God slavering for sex. Priests enthusiastically copulating with street prostitutes? Nuns moaning in orgasmic bliss, begging for more, during a twenty-man gangbang? This was just what Farringworth needed for his plan, and it was exactly what he was getting thanks to the Metopronil.

Oh, the wonder of pharmaceutical science...

John watched, fascinated, as the nun grinned lasciviously through what must be incalculable pain.

Her eyes were glazed in lust as the freak's turgid flesh split her wide and punched up into her bowels, bruising internal organs. John could see the remnants of her reason shutting down, a lust-crazed insanity replacing it. All will was lost in this nun now. Her faith too was lost, abandoned. A rosary still hung down between her tightly wrapped breasts swaying back and forth to the rhythm of the monster's pelvic thrusts.

Her name was Mother Angelina and she was very nearly a living saint. Her humanitarian efforts with AIDS and Ebola victims in Southern Africa were known all over the globe. She'd negotiated peace talks with terrorists and even traded herself for the release of hostages. Just last week she'd addressed the United Nations to plead for an end to the war in the Middle East. And now this sainted woman, revered all over the globe, was taking inch after inch of gnarled cock flesh between her flabby ass cheeks and loving every minute of it.

Cameras in each corner of the ceiling were recording her every moan and shriek. John smiled and winked at his beautiful monster who was obviously having the time of his life. From deep beneath his Cro-Magnon brow Billy winked back. John hoped that his cameras would record the exact moment when Mother Angelina's mind flew asunder. He wanted it all—every second—for the feed they piped anonymously onto the internet. Later, Michaels would shoot her full of heroin and dump her off on a street corner in San Francisco's Tenderloin district with the transvestites and prostitutes or in the middle of Time's Square or even on The Las Vegas Strip. He had the resources to put her anywhere in the world. In a donkey show in Tijuana, in Hong Kong in one of the Filipino brothels in Lan Kwai Fong. He could dress her in a French maid's outfit and drop her in Bangkok, in Pat Pong where Thai girls shot ping-pong balls out of their vaginas with overdeveloped kegel muscles. No matter where she ended up, her days as an inspiration to millions were over. When this tape hit the streets it would shake the faith of half the world. Then God would have to come to him. He would have to reveal himself in all his flawed and imperfect glory and John would capture him like a firefly in a jar. Then he'd have all the power he needed to make the angels love him.

Farringworth's last glimpse of the scene was this: Mother changing positions, her tits hanging. She was fellating Billy's waste-smeared cock with gusto, leaving brown marks around her mouth like a sloppy child eating a chocolate ice-cream cone.

The billionaire eased the door quietly shut and relocked it. He then continued next door to the suite where his beautiful angels lived.

The angles were John Farringworth's first acquisitions. They were twins, lithe and elegant giants nearly seven feet tall, albinos, hermaphrodites, gaunt as scarecrows. Niveous elongated forms so achromatic they were nearly transparent. Ethereal wraiths wrapped in paper-thin white skin that appeared to be little more than a sheer blanket draped over their wiry muscles. Their eyes were as cold and bloodless as their flesh, utterly devoid of pigmentation save for the pinhole-sized pupils. Long spidery fingers ending in nails, so overgrown that they curled under at the ends and spiraled, dominated their hands. They refused to let them be clipped. Their hair was likewise overgrown. Spilling in long luxurious locks down their backs to the tops of their upturned buttocks. Their sexual organs, both male and female, were not the half-formed diminutive aberrations found on most beings of combined genders. They had long fully formed penises that hung down over perfectly shaped and fully functional vaginas. When erect their enormous members were nearly as long as a baby's arm and just as thick. Their grapefruit sized breasts were the only hints of adipose tissue on their otherwise anemic forms. John longed to suckle at those luscious tits but his attempts to do so had all ended poorly.

The angels had been conjoined hip to hip right up until their twelfth birthday when they were surgically separated, not at birth but at puberty, right when they had needed each other the most. The arm that they had shared was left on the operating table and a scar zig-zagged from hip to shoulder as a memento of the union they once shared. They never spoke and rarely even acknowledged the existence of other human beings. They lived in their own world where they were the sole citizenries. Any attempt to enter their reality was aggressively, violently repelled. John had been trying for years.

He crept up to their door and was both excited and disappointed to hear the sounds of passion emanating from within. He slipped the key into the lock and ducked into the poshly decorated suite where he kept his lovely angels caged. The moans and sighs and musky sent of lovemaking came from the living room and John tip-toed over to peer across the couch where Enoch and Hosea lay opposite each other, one's head meeting the other's feet, so that their confusion of sex organs lined up perfectly, vagina to penis, allowing them both to fuck even while being fucked.

Farrington watched the twin angel's impossibly long cocks, both at least 14 inches in length, slide in and out of the hairy pink apertures that lay tucked between their marble thighs. They sucked on one other's yard-long toes and moaned and shivered as they copulated in long salacious strokes. The billionaire ran his eyes over them in envy as his angels rode rippling waves of mutual ecstasy to a heaven that he could only dream of.

Enoch and Hosea sped up their rhythm until their enormous members were pounding in and out of each other's sopping wet vaginas with violent enthusiasm. Their eyes betrayed an almost religious rapture, as they were simultaneously impaled on the long, venous, blood-gorged cocks. They began to shriek in agony/ecstasy, as a convulsive orgasm ripped through them, wracking their bodies with spasms so intense that it seemed it would break them apart.

They detached from one another. John watched in shocked delight as Enoch slid down his sibling's body until Hosea's genitals were pressed against his pale lips and Enoch's pulsating cock slipped down his brother's throat. Farrington shuddered and grabbed hold of his throbbing erection as Enoch began licking his own vaginal juices from his brother's cock then slid his tongue up inside his brother's wet silken crevice to lap his own semen from its sweet slippery folds. Farrington began vigorously masturbating, watching this bizarre and sensuous dance of flesh and fluid. Farrington's own cock looked weak and pathetic in comparison to the magnificent organs wielded by the megalomorphic twins.

The incestuous angels sucked and licked each other back to full erections and then to yet another shudder-some orgasm, which they both eagerly swallowed, drinking down their identical DNA in great gulps as if to spill any of it would have been to lose something of themselves. They rose from the couch with their faces glazed with semen and vaginal fluids just as Farrington ejaculated onto the couch where they had lain. Their eyes met and the angels charged in a frenzy of rage. Farrington was just fast enough to reach the door and lock it behind him before the angels could seize him and tear him apart. He leaned against the heavy steel door breathing hard as the twin hermaphrodites raged on the other side. If they had caught him they would've killed him for what he had witnessed, for interrupting their tender moment, but Farrington would not give them the chance... not yet.

Farrington was still aroused. His cock bulged out in front of him looking swollen and furious. His own mounting temper trembled through him, making his entire body shake. He did everything for them but still the angels rebuked him.

A sob caught in his throat and three angry tears squeezed out from the corners of his eyes, leaving warm salty trails down his cheeks as they slid down to moisten his lips. He looked like a spoiled child. The billionaire strode down the hall and wrenched open the monster's door. Mother Angelina was still there in Billy's room, now gagging on his monstrous hog-leg thick organ.

There was a pole draped across her shoulders to which her wrists had been handcuffed. She was on her knees staring up at the hideous abomination with the mastodon head as he vigorously raped her esophagus. Billy turned and smiled. All two hundred plus teeth—an affliction called excessive dentition—beamed gleefully at the perverse billionaire as he stepped into the room with his erection leading the way.

Farrington walked up behind Billy and began caressing the massive protrusions of bone and flesh that bulged from his warped spine. He slathered a finger in saliva and slipped it into the monster's rectum then began sliding it in and out. He spit into his other palm and then lubricated his cock. Billy shuddered in ecstasy and sped up the rhythm of his cock in the sainted mother's throat as the billionaire squeezed his erection into the monster's anus.

Taking out his vexations on Billy's asshole, he leaned over the monster's shoulder to look down at Mother Angelina. In spite of the obvious torment, her eyes looked greedy in perverse desire as her mouth stretched wide to accommodate the unnatural girth of Billy's freakish sex organ.

"I bet you think you're in hell," Farrington said as he thrust his cock deep into Billy's asshole, which simultaneously forced Billy's cock deeper into Mother Angelina's throat.

"But of course this isn't hell. This is earth, the earth your god created, and this demon is one of God's creatures. Show us your altruism now. Let's see God's little whore demonstrate her humanitarianism on my beautiful monster's cock…"

Farrington fucked Billy harder and soon the monster was cumming hard in the nun's vandalized throat. It bubbled up out of her mouth and spilled down her chin and between her massive breasts. Farrington removed his cock from Billy's rectum as the monster squeezed out the last of his vile seed onto the nun's wrinkled forehead. Taking his shit-slickened erection in hand he seized the nun's head and forced it between her lips. It took only a few strokes before he ejaculated as well. He withdrew his cock from her mouth as the first tremors of orgasm ripped through him, leaving a trail of the monster's fecal matter smeared across her lips. He then aimed his cock between her eyes and bathed her face with his semen.

"This is my body! This is my blood!" he shrieked as his penis spurted out streams of warm semen onto her cheeks and eyelashes. Then he and Billy began urinating all over her. Their golden shower rained down over her like baptismal waters. Billy reached out one of his massive hands and seized Mother Angelina's jaw, forcing it open wider so that Farrington could piss down her throat.

"Show yourself! Show yourself to me! How many of your slaves do I have to humiliate before you will face me?" The billionaire screamed at the empty air as he drowned the old nun in urine. He didn't notice Michaels creep in behind him until he felt the man's rough hands on his shoulders.

"Your guests have arrived."

"What? Oh, the journalists..."

"Yes. We have to clean you up and get you ready."

Michaels leaned down and licked the remaining semen and feces from his employer's cock. Not to be outdone, Billy reached down and yanked the nun's over-sized breasts out of their latex bustier, squeezing them so tightly in his hands that they began turning purple, and lifted her off the floor by them, nearly ripping her tremendous mammary glands right off her chest. He then licked the semen, feces, and urine off her face with a tongue as long and thick as a sea slug. Michaels looked at the hideous freak that was now grinning at Farrington as if awaiting his approval for his little show of affection and shook his head in disgust. He then turned and led his demented employer out of the room and down the hall.

"I just don't understand you, sir. What is it you see in these monsters? And why this obsession with God? What do the two have to do with each other?" Michaels was clearly disturbed by what he had seen.

"The freaks are but a means to an end, Michaels."

"But to what end? Just so you can humiliate the church?"

"Don't you see? I want to understand God, to usurp his power. I'm not the first person to assert that the only way to know God is through his works, his creations. Buddhists contemplate nature's wonders, streams and flowers. Scientists study natural disasters and the vast expanses of inner and outer space. They study the most awe-inspiring aspect of creation. I've studied it as well. Everything from nucleotides to quasars. I've spent hours in Tibetan monasteries watching snowflakes accumulate on a hillside. And yes, I have been awed by it all. Like all of them, awed stupid. But I have come to no greater understanding of perfection. So now I study not God's perfection but his flaws. I study his mistakes." He gestured toward Betty who was just leaving the pool house, undulating her gelatinous form down the hallway toward her room. Her hideously obese body a riot of ripples and waves as she moved by the momentum of her own corpulent rolls flopping in a worm-like crawl.

"And what better way to know God's creations than in the biblical sense?"

"I get that part. I think. But what about the priests and nuns?"

"Oh, that you will understand soon enough."

They walked past the angel's suite and John Farrington stopped, staring at the door.

"Sir, we have guests. We can't keep them waiting."

Farrington's voice sounded very far away. Was there a tear in his eye? "Why don't they love me Michaels? Why?"

(III)

James Bryant and Richard Westmore sat on a leather couch longer than either of their apartments and soft as foreskin. They stared at the travertine marble floors that shined like glass, the faux finished walls trimmed in mahogany, the huge round stained glass skylight, and the solid granite, stainless steel, tumbled marble, and oak, cherry and rose wood furniture that all seemed to have come from an art gallery rather than a furniture showroom. Everything in the room was brand new and expensive. Bryant noticed right away that there was not a single picture or personal artifact in the room. He'd been expecting to see the obligatory self-portrait over the mantle but this room was completely depersonalized. Anyone could have lived here. Anyone with a nine figure financial portfolio.

"I guess this guy isn't into antiques huh?" Westmore said as he began snapping pictures of the room.

"If I didn't know better I'd think he just bought all this furniture before we arrived. It even smells new." Bryant replied.

"And it's uncomfortable as hell!" Westmore grumbled nearly falling out of a hand-carved marble chair with no seat cushion and a back that rose higher than a man's head.

Bryant was about to speak again when his ears caught a commotion out in the hallway.

Westmore and Bryant turned to look out into the main foyer where Michaels was wrestling a tall well-built and naked gentleman up the stairs. The man was obviously distraught and kept crying out—something about angels. It sounded like "Why don't the angels love me?" Finally the naked lunatic collapsed into Michaels arms in tears and allowed himself to be led upstairs and into one of the many second floor bedrooms.

Westmore began, "You don't think that's—"

"It better not be," Bryant offered, shaking his head in incredulity. "If that was Farrington, we've got a major basket case on our hands."

"Thank God you're the one doing the writing." Westmore frowned around the room until he noticed an ashtray on a side table. "I think my karma's kicking in again. We haven't been here twenty minutes, and things are already fucked up. And I can tell you right now; this is going to take longer than we thought. I'm gonna miss the fuckin' Yankees' game."

"We don't get paid by the hour. What happened to your work ethic?"

Westmore tapped an ash. "What work ethic? And where's the British guy? We're in a billionaire's house. You'd think the Brit would at least offer us a drink."

Bryant walked around the spacious room, jotting down descriptive notes. "You've had enough to drink. Why don't you just chill and take some pictures. You're griping like some woman on the rag."

"Gimme a break. The cramps are really bad today, makes me bitchy." But he knew he really should get more shots of the interior. He walked to the plate-glass window overlooking n elaborate garden. He touched the glass.

"This isn't glass."

"What?" Bryant said, seeming annoyed.

"It's Lexan or something, something polycarbonate. Stuff they use in banks 'cos it's bulletproof. Won't break."

"I'll remind you that the owner is a billionaire. He can afford security measures like that."

Now Westmore tested the knobs on the French doors. They were key-locked. He came back and crushed his cigarette out but suddenly found his hands shaking. "Fuck."

Bryant couldn't help but notice. "You're not old enough to have the shakes. Think it might be a good idea to quit drinking?"

Westmore felt strange, as he had at the airport bar. He felt as though some aspect of his spirit had abandoned him, but why? What was it fleeing? "I just got that bad feeling again. Bad vibes."

"Well, get a hold of yourself." Next, Bryant rolled his eyes at the cigarette smoldering in the tray. "That's not an ashtray, Westmore. It's a Hummel pit dish, probably cost a thousand dollars."

"Fuck," Westmore said. Next, an inexplicable impulse caused him to turn. The furthest corner of the room stood dark. He thought he'd seen someone standing there, but when he squinted, it was just grainy dark.

Bryant smiled. "You're really a screw-loose."

"And you know something else?" Westmore scratched his beard. "This Brit, this Micheals guy, *he* could be Farrington for all we know."

"I assure you I'm not, Mr. Westmore."

The tall British manservant was right behind Westmore when he turned back toward the foyer. The photographer jumped back with a start at the sudden proximity of the man.

"Jesus, man!"

Michaels sighed when he noticed the cigarette butt in the pit dish. "Please, gentlemen. Sit. I'll have someone bring you some tea, or, if you'd prefer—"

Westmore perked up.

"—The armoire is actually a liquor cabinet."

Westmore walked immediately to the high, polished armoire near the arched doorway.

"Mr. Farrington will be with you soon," Michaels continued in the clipped accent. He seemed distant, or distracted. "I have to go see to another guest who has just arrived."

"That wasn't Mr. Farrington blubbering on your shoulder just now in his birthday suit was it?" Westmore asked.

"Please, have a seat. I will be back momentarily." Michaels disappeared into another room leaving the two journalists alone again.

"You have a way with words," Bryant said. "A bad way."

Westmore shrugged. When he opened the armoire, he found racks of top shelf liquor. He picked up a bottle, impressed. "To hell with Bud Light. This guy's got Macallen and Johnny Walker Blue!"

"I think the naked guy *was* Farrington," Bryant said. "Michaels really seemed out of it, didn't he? Like he was bothered, or embarrassed."

"Yeah, or maybe he's just a flake. Who cares? At least I'm not missing the Yankees for nothing." He poured himself a drink and pointed to the liquor rack. "What do you want?"

"Proper liver function." Then Bryant noticed that the coffee table in front of the couch was now laid out with hors d'oeuvres. Someone must have brought them in while they were busy watching the man on the stairs have a nervous breakdown.

"This is some spread," Westmore observed. He snapped a picture, then they both sat back down and began to eat: toast points with smoked salmon and capers, Beluga caviar with sour cream, green onions, and boiled egg, crab-filled mushroom caps, and garlic butter dipped escargot. They had no idea what half the stuff they were eating was but it all tasted wonderful. Westmore downed two more scotches in the process.

They had just finished off the last of the caviar when a handsome, well-groomed young man in an Armani suit sat down across from them in a huge stainless steel chair they had both thought was a modern art sculpture.

"Welcome gentleman. I trust you enjoyed your snack? My name is John Farrington."

It was the same man who'd been crying in Michaels's arms. Only now, in his $10,000 power suit, he looked anything but vulnerable. In fact, he looked invincible. His eyes shone with a feral predatory intelligence as if he were preparing to attack and was just trying to decide which of them was the fittest and which one the gene pool could do without. They seemed to be scouring the two reporters for weaknesses.

Both Bryant and Westmore were caught in a moment of silence, looking up. Then they both rose.

"My name is James Bryant and this is Richard Westmore. We're here to interview you for *Blue Chip* magazine. Do you mind if my partner here gets a few photos of you for the cover?"

They shook hands and then settled back down onto the plush sofa. Westmore remained standing and began loading film into his Nikon 35mm.

"Very pleased to meet you gentlemen and I'm sorry but I will have to insist that you do not photograph me."

The two journalists were shocked.

"What? No photos?"

"You may take photographs of my home and property but I'm afraid no pictures of me."

"But why? I thought it was all arranged?" Westmore practically shrieked as he saw his assignment slipping out of his control.

"I am a very private man. I don't wish to become the type of person who cannot go anywhere without a battalion of bodyguards to protect me from beggars, kidnappers and paparazzi. I'm sure you understand."

"No, I don't fucking understand!" Westmore was buzzed, irritation mixing with the scotch. It was not a positive combination. Bryant seized his partner's wrist and pulled him back down onto the couch.

"Excuse my friend here. He's enjoyed your hospitality a little too much I'm afraid. The alcohol is affecting his manners. We're happy to respect your wishes, Mr. Farrington."

Farrington smiled; clearly amused at the reaction he was having on his guests.

"No excuses necessary. I understand that it is highly unusual to not be able to photograph the subject of your story."

"Damn right it's highly unusual," Westmore muttered. "What do you want on your lead-page? A picture of the pool, or the foyer?"

Bryant once more clamped a hand on his partner's

shoulder in an attempt to calm him but Westmore shrugged it off. Farrington leaned forward with a leering grin scarring his movie star face. His eyes bored into Westmore's as if he were trying to see through to his soul.

"May I ask you a question?"

"Well, I guess that's fair." Bryant replied, anything to change the subject.

"Do you believe in God?"

The question startled the two reporters and immediately they recalled the bizarre words the billionaire had shouted as Michaels had attempted to drag him up the stairs to his bedroom. It was something like: "Why don't the angels love me?" Bryant began to wonder if the billionaire was some type of religious fanatic.

"Now what the hell does that have to do with us taking pictures or how you managed to become the world's youngest self-made billionaire? That *is* our assignment, you know. Financial strategies, business plans, a little background info for filler."

"Actually it has everything to do with it, Mr. Westmore. Now please, humor me."

"Well... Okay... No. I don't believe in God," Bryant said. "I don't believe in anything. I either know or I do not know."

"A very admirable yet difficult stance. I wonder how that's working out for you?"·

"Well as a matter of fact I do just—"

Farrington cut him off before he could finish his sentence.

"And what about you, Mr. Westmore? Do you believe?"

Westmore diddled with an unlit cigarette. "I'm a Christian, if that's what you mean. Not a very good one, mind you." He paused. "Correction, I'm an *existential* Christian, a Kierkegaardist."

"Fine, but you do believe in the all-mighty, the all-perfect, the all-knowing, and omni-benevolent?"

"Sure."

Farrington chuckled under his breath and rolled his eyes up toward the ceiling.

"Do you even know what that means? Do you even have the slightest concept of what perfection is?"

"I'm sorry but I don't know what you're getting at exactly," Bryant poised.

"I believe in God as well, Mr. Bryant. I believe that he is real and alive and that man was created in his image. All that I do so shall ye also do and more than that shall ye also do. Christ said those words and I believe they are prophetic. I believe that he was saying that we all have the power of a God within us. And I mean to claim that power."

"And how the hell do you mean to do that?" Westmore was starting to sober rapidly as he began to realize that the man they were sent to interview, the man who had made hundreds of millions in less than half a decade of trading, just might be out of his mind.

"I thought you were the journalist, Mr. Bryant? Your photographer seems to be asking all the questions."

"Like I said, he is a tad drunk."

"No matter. You asked a very good question Mr. Westmore and it deserves a very good answer. I intend to capture God."

That sobered him up even more. Westmore and Bryant stared at the billionaire with their jaws hanging open.

"Very intriguing." Bryant replied.

"Intriguing? It's ridiculous! How the hell do you intend to capture God?"

The billionaire rose from his seat and turned his back to the two reporters.

"You see, gentlemen, all my life everything I've ever put my mind to I've accomplished and generally with relative ease. I have run ultra-marathon's, won hundred mile bike races and triathlons, climbed mountains, trekked across deserts, and made billions of dollars. I am the ultimate perfectionist yet if God exists than he would be the ultimate archetype of perfection. The only way to be truly perfect would be to be exactly like God. But it's a perfection so absolute as to be unimaginable. You see, man cannot truly fathom perfection. We have no reference point with which to form even the most fundamental concept of it."

He picked a bible up off an end table on the opposite end of the sofa and threw it into the fireplace where it was immediately consumed.

"It's not in here," he said.

He picked up a copy of the Torah and threw that in as well, then the Bhagavad-Gita, the Koran, the Book of Mormon, the I Ching, the Tao Te Ching. All of them he tossed into the fire.

"It's not in here. Not in here or here. Everything in life is flawed and corrupted and so God remains an enigma. All our attempts to capture him in literature, philosophy, and religion have amounted to little more than childish fantasies and superstitions based on our fears and desires. Garbage. All of it."

The two reporters stared at the young billionaire as he paced the polished marble floor, gesticulating madly.

"It's like trying to imagine a shape or color you've never seen and then to recreate it on canvas. It can't be done."

Bryant suddenly understood what the man was getting at. "But once you've seen that color. I mean, once you've seen God…"

"Well, once I have a true and accurate image of perfection, of something utterly without flaw, then as with everything else in my life, if I can conceive it then I can achieve it."

"Okay, then how do you plan to get God to reveal himself to you?"

"That I shall explain later, but right now it's getting late. I'll have Michaels show you to your rooms. We can discuss it further at dinner."

"But we've got a flight out tonight," Westmore interjected, "and a deadline tomorrow!"

"Your deadline's been extended," Farringworth informed, "and your plans altered slightly. You'll be staying at my home for several days. It's already been cleared by your editor." Farringworth was walking away, heels snapping on the tile floor. "Feel free to call him and verify." Then he was gone.

"This is fucked up," Westmore nearly yelled. "Call the office on your cell."

"I am, I am." Bryant was dialing, waiting. "And I'll admit, this is pretty weird."

"Weird? It's a Chinese fuckin' fire drill. It's FUCKED UP."

Bryant was talking, nodding. His brow rose, then he turned the phone off. "Farringworth wasn't kidding. Tait just told me everything's clear. Wants us to stay up to a week, get the article right."

"Good luck." Westmore was pouring another scotch. "And like I said, it's a damn good thing you're the writer here. Better you than me, man. Have fun interviewing a guy who thinks he can *capture God.*" Westmore couldn't reserve his laughter. He meandered to the window again, and the French doors, and just when he was starting to calm down, his heart lurched. Michaels was standing right next to him, hands behind his back, smiling very faintly. It was as though he'd materialized from the air.

"I think you'll find Mr. Farringworth a most interesting interview subject."

"You ain't kidding."

"Finish your drink, then I'll take you to your rooms. I think you'll find them adequate."

"I'm sure we will," Bryant said. "And I agree, Mr. Farringworth is a *very* interesting man."

Westmore was staring into more distraction. Unconsciously, he put his hand on the knob to the French doors, attempted to open them, then remembered they were locked. "Your grounds must be crawling with security and alarm sensors. Why are the doors locked?"

Michaels maintained the trace smile. "A common sense precaution. There are many valuables in this house, Mr. Westmore."

Sure, but... Westmore didn't finish the thought. The vibes were bugging him again. Outside, beyond the extensive garden, he could see the cul-de-sac in front of the next wing of the mansion. A panel van drove by, with the letters DAYE PHARMACEUTICALS, LTD along the side.

Bryant saw it too. "I don't remember anything in the

profile about Mr. Farringworth owning a drug company."

"He doesn't own it. He merely has an esoteric interest in one."

"Esoteric?" Bryant shot him a puzzled look. "You mean financial."

"I mean esoteric."

But Westmore wasn't listening. Instead his fingers were touching the window, not glass but something composite. "These windows are Lexan, aren't they?"

"Yes, they are, Mr. Westmore. Appearance is important, especially to a man such as Mr. Farringworth, but security is equally important. Every window in the mansion is Lexan—it was very expensive. And you're correct, the mansion as well as the grounds are extensively alarmed. Every door is secured by an electronic lock system. We don't want anybody getting in."

Or out, Westmore thought.

(IV)

Fadden was not familiar with such anomalies but if he had been?

The genetic disorders were multifarious: entropy of the digits, supernumerary thumb, and, above all, unilateral hemihypertropy with congenital asymmetry, not to mention acute hyperpituitaryism. The woman on the bed's name was Carol, though her name was as useless as her life. She was twenty-nine years old but she had the face of a ten-year-old, and the basic body growth of one. *Basic* body growth. That was it. The hemihypertrophy had caused half of her four-foot six frame to grow faster than the other half. Right leg and arm were twice the girth of the left, and several inches longer. Her thumbs were as large as bratwursts, while her remaining fingers had stopped growing when she was five. Even at almost thirty, though, she looked like a little monster child.

Fadden cursed himself, humping the woman/child so hard he was nearly bending her ruined body in half. He didn't want to do this.

He couldn't help it.

Pieces of reason sliced through his mindless lust. Fadden was a priest as well as the spiritual counselor for the White House Chaplain Unit. In a sense—a diocesan one—he was quite famous, having provided psychological counseling and spiritual guidance for three presidents and innumerable high-echelon executive personnel. He'd been celibate for his entire life, a faithful steward of God.

Now that same steward was frenetically copulating with a grievously defected invalid. And he couldn't get enough. He'd come three times already, and was going again, shuddering as Carol's sausage-sized thumb roved in his rectum. Fadden didn't remember how he'd gotten here, and after they'd forced him to swallow the pink pill, he didn't care. His lust raged and would not abate. Every conscious minute—or second—made him aware of this most grueling of sins. But he couldn't stop. If he kept it up at this rate, he'd have a heart attack—in fact, part of him *wanted* to have a heart attack. If felt as though death was the only thing that could turn off the lust and arousal.

Another of Carol's anomalies was called transverse vaginal septism. She had, essentially, two vaginal canals packed into the confines of one. Fadden's cock traded from one canal to the other, with frequency. Evidently, they'd given the woman one of those pills too, because, in spite of this heinous abuse, she couldn't get enough, and if she were able to talk, that's what she'd be crying out for: more.

Fadden gave her more.

For quite a while.

A moment before his crisis, he was able to withdraw, then jumped up, slipped his penis into her mouth, and came. His heart skipped beats, his exhaustion crushed him, and his sperm seemed to slide out of his cock like a warm worm. Carol gulped the worm down greedily, bucking as she masturbated with the shit-smudged thumb.

God Almighty, what is wrong with me? He could scarcely move, so instead he lay back, his crotch to the girl's face, gasping. *Give me strength.* If God couldn't give it to him, who could? He knew he'd need it from somewhere. Fadden was spent, drained, wrecked by fatigue…yet still erect, desires still raging. It was only a minute ago that he'd ejaculated, and now he wanted to go again. He *needed* to go again.

Forgive me, God. I can't help it. Forgive me…

The giant thumb bridged his cock, while her tiny fingers tickled his testicles. Soon the testicles were in her mouth, being sucked.

Fadden felt mindless, buried in sin, in evil. That's what was going on here, surely. Why were they doing this to him? What other explanation could there be?

He let the queer little girl mouth give succor to his balls for a time more, while he just stared off. Across the room was another bed, where a Hasidic rabbi groaned, sodomizing some bent-up thing that appeared to be female. Her limbs seemed...bowed, and she panted like a dog as the rabbi plungered her rectum...

Good God...

Mounted on the ceiling, he could see, cameras focused down, catching every angle of the demented festivities taking place on the beds. What where they doing here?

And who were *they?*

Fadden couldn't contemplate these reasonable questions for much longer. His lust was burning him down now. He forced his previously celibate cock down to her tonsils, sighed, then slid down and was in her vagina again—or one of the vaginas.

He would fuck Carol four more times tonight, and then die of a massive myocardial infarction. A digital film of his sexual foray would hit the internet and major network news affiliations within twenty-four hours.

His body would never be found.

(V)

Westmore woke at about three a.m. Sat bolt upright, sweating. This had been happening with some frequency of late—forty now, and no life but his work, and "downing" a few *after* work, or "Let's go have a few beers." A "few" would always be eight or ten. He knew he was at least a borderline drunk but never consciously admitted that. All photographers drank—all good ones, at any rate. That was his excuse. But the booze always screwed up his sleep.

When he'd jerked awake, he'd been terrified: some

creepy impression that someone else was in the room. In fact he even thought he'd seen a shape standing there in the particulate darkness, looking down at him in bed. He'd nearly cried out, snapping on the light.

No one was there, of course, but did he hear a mutter just as he'd turned on the light? He thought he'd heard someone say, distinctly: "Shit. I hate light."

He felt imbecilic at once. It was those Johnny Walker Blues he'd slugged down earlier—strong stuff. *I'm gonna quit drinking,* he resolved, rubbing his eyes.

The room looked like the presidential suite at the Four Seasons. Hot tub, home theater, inlaid paneled walls, four-poster bed. The plush Kashmiri carpet probably cost more than Westmore's puissant condo. Like downstairs, two French doors faced east; they led to a balcony, over-looking the garden, and a sedate moon shone through the door's multiple square panes. A cigarette on the balcony sounded great but when he tested the door's knobs, they were locked. He touched the panes. Lexan.

Stop being paranoid, he thought. Now, if the *bedroom's* door was locked, he might have a right to be paranoid, but the door clicked open when he tried it. He felt weird and hung over. Hair of the dog was always the worst excuse, but the Johnny Blue was *good* scotch. He'd thrown his clothes over the teal récamier couch against a wall decorated by what appeared to be an original Rothko. The abstract painting reminded him of a long lost love—a girl he'd loved more than anything but never told—which only soured his mood further. Failure was everywhere he looked. Despair was every-where, to the extent that he felt at home in it. He hur-riedly pulled his clothes back on, grabbed his cigarettes, and left the room.

Yeah, I'll quit drinking some day... Just not today.

The main upstairs hall stood morgue-silent and dark. From the railing, which stretched before the guest rooms, he looked across the atrium-like foyer and remembered more detail of the mansion's layout. Another hallway could be seen just across the way, and he presumed there were more guest rooms there too—or perhaps Farringworth's bedroom. Had it really been Farrington himself that they'd seen earlier in the same hallway, naked, weeping? *Something about angels,* Westmore remembered. Then all that whacked out talk about conceptions of perfection, and God. *What a kook...*

He took the sweeping steps down quietly as he could. His headache stalked him. Downstairs, only a few lights were on, in the main foyer. He slipped back into the parlor where they'd first met Farringworth and was immediately at the armoire. Bottles clinked as he withdrew the Johnny Blue. He poured himself two fingers, then hunted for whatever that thing was that Bryant said wasn't really an ashtray.

A clock ticked somewhere deeper in the house. He was looking out the Lexan panels of the French doors, into the garden. Thinking, thinking.

What was this place? What was Farringworth really all about? And that British guy? The first drink went fast, yet left him keenly focused. *Why doesn't he want pictures? Why would he even consent to an interview?* He never had in the past. *And what about that—*

A car motor started outside, lights popped on. Another one of those panel vans drove out of the cul-de-sac: DAYE PHARMACEUTICALS, LTD.

What's with that shit? What's with drug company

vans driving around this ritzy joint at three in the morning?

The van's red taillights faded, then winked out. The silence now seemed to amplify; Westmore could hear things beyond it: house noises, the a/c whispering. The clock—wherever it was—sounded louder, its tick more crisp. Then he stiffened. Had he heard a moan? A voice? From somewhere—deep, deep in the house. A door clicked opened and closed. Footsteps. Then nothing.

The vibes were raging.

Bad vibes.

Westmore smoked in the dark, had another scotch. The booze and cigarettes were wearing him out. *Life* was wearing him out. *Wear me out some more,* he pleaded. *Just fuckin' take me. Wear me out till there's nothing left...*

He was getting drunk again. Was it God he was pleading to, the God he claimed to believe in? *God doesn't do shit for me, but...why should He? I don't deserve it.* But what about Bryant? What about that kook Farringworth and that fruitcake Michaels? Did God have different conceptions of different people? He must. Everyone truly wasn't the same, and no culture was the same. There were too many variables. Therefore one god could not save all. *God must have many faces,* Westmore considered, the scotch heating his insides.

Let's have one more drink, just you and me, okay, God?

Tipsiness urged him to walk more carefully back to the armoire, but not carefully enough because—

Smack!

—he'd forgotten than he'd left the armoire's teakwood door hanging open, and he walked right into it, forehead to edge. Pain seemed to bite him like a lunging animal. He had time to think, *What a drunken asshole,* then brought his hands to his head and collapsed.

He blacked in and out. Blood from the gash leaked into his eyes; now the pain was like a piton driven into his forehead. He lay there for a moment, head beating. Was he seriously hurt? Wasn't that how William Holden had died? Hit his head drunk, then bled to death because the alcohol thinned his blood. *Fuck,* Westmore managed to think. At least his was on par. When he tried to lean up, the pain slammed him back down, like a foot to his chest.

Squinting, dizzy, he saw a shadow before him. *Must be the shadow of the armoire door,* he thought. But it wasn't.

The shadow leaned over.

"Michaels?" he murmured. It must be Michaels.

"No," the shadow said. A man's voice but...strange. The voice seemed echoic and dark yet radiant at the same time—an impossible description. The shadow was...

What the fuck is he doing? Mugging me?

The shadow's hand was on his shirt. It withdrew his pack of cigarettes and lighter.

A snap, a brief flame. The shadow was standing upright again, looking around; Westmore could tell where the person was looking by the lit end of the cigarette.

Smoke creamed before its face, and the strange voice resounded again: "How would I know that your birth mother walked out of the hospital the day you were born? How would I know you almost got run down by Mrs. Korella, in her VW bug, on Stonybrook drive, the day after Kennedy was shot, and you shit your pants? How would I know you used to lust after women in church when you were an acolyte?" A pause, and the impression of a smile. "Gotta admit, some of those chicks were hot—but it's still lust, and lust is selfish. It's a piss-ant sin."

Westmore's voice groaned like old wood. "Who are you?"

"My name is a cabalistic secret. I can't tell you. My name is a word that you are not capable of calculating."

Westmore dragged himself up to sit slumped at the long table. The man stood at the other end; moonlight lit half of his face like foxfire. Westmore shook his head to try and clear his vision.

"Your name is...*what?*"

"I'm an angel. That's all you need to know."

Westmore slumped further. *Great. Have another drink, Westmore.*

"You don't believe me?" The cigarette tip brightened momentarily, then more smoke floated. "How else would I know those things? Remember the guy you wanted to kill in the Army, behind the Bravo Company barracks? He called you a pussy, so you fought him. You wanted to kill him, Westmore. And you were *gonna* kill him, too, weren't you? Remember?"

Westmore felt sick. He did remember.

"But you didn't do it. Why didn't you?"

Westmore stared as much at the shadow as he did into the past. "I changed my mind."

"Wrong. Wanna know why you didn't?"

"Why?"

"Because of me. I was the whisper in your ear. I was your good judgment."

"Really?" Westmore chuckled under his breath. *I'm hallucinating, fine. I understand now. I can understand that.* Yet he challenged the mirage. "Why would you do that? Why would you whisper that in my ear?"

"Because you don't need murder on your track-record of sin. You're in deep enough shit already, I can tell you that, asshole."

"Great language for an angel," the photographer retorted.

"Hey, God doesn't give a shit about that. It's all about what's here"—the angel touched his head—"and here"—the angel touched his heart—"and how you use that out there." The angel pointed to the window.

Another drag on the cigarette. Westmore squinted more details; his eyes were acclimating. The "angel" wore dark jeans and a black t-shirt that read, in white block letters: *ZZLSEN.* He had long straight hair, like someone in a metal band, a handsome, rugged face.

"You're not an angel, you're just some fuckin' guy."

The figure nodded, and then sipped Westmore's scotch.

"And, besides," the photographer added, "angels don't drink scotch or smoke Marlboros."

"Why not? I indulge every hundred years or so—I think I've earned it."

"But I thought the body is a temple of the lord."

"It is, asshole—to *you.* But I'm immune. I'm a higher being." Another sip, and he put the glass down. "Johnny Blue's no big deal. Next one, pour some Macallan." The angel took a step closer, face out of the moonlight. "Listen, and listen good. This is how we do things. You don't understand, but listen anyway. I'm from an offshoot order of the Seraphim—I'm called a

Caliginaut. Angels from my order willingly descend from the rapture. We're, like, God's recon crew, his commandos. We condition ourselves to darkness. We're...*special* angels."

"Where are your wings? Angels have wings."

"We cut them off ourselves, by the decree of our order. It's a sacrifice, Westmore. We have to do it ourselves, it's gnarly." The angel stepped closer to the French doors, turned, and peeled his t-shirt up. "My attentor joints. See?"

Westmore saw, almost wincing. Two flesh-covered stumps protruded from a y-shaped ridge on his back. "You amputate your own wings is what you're telling me?"

"Yeah. We use a tool called a Skttaz, like a giant pair of bolt cutters, man. It's hardcore."

Westmore felt winded; he dabbed at the gash on his head with a handkerchief. He pushed past the pain, though, and played along with the illusion. "What kind of a God would expect such a thing? What kind of a God would be appeased by an act like that?"

"He's not appeased. He doesn't want us to do it but we do it anyway, because there's nothing else we CAN do. It's a gesture. It's the only way we can acknowledge our unworthiness in His eyes."

Unworthiness, Westmore thought.

The angel was leaning over, right in front of Westmore now. "Still don't believe me, huh? There's so little faith anymore. Remember when that kid Nathan beat you up for stealing his army men? Remember when you and Dougie made the crippled kid cry? You stole his book bag. Fourth grade, Summerset Elementary School. How could I know that?"

"It's easy," Westmore countered. "You're a hallucination, born of my mind. I drank too much and now I'm seeing things."

"Maybe you're right. If you died, right now, you'd go to hell. Be careful."

"But isn't hell really just death?"

"Yes," the angel said. The distant clock ticked through a long pause. "And no, not at all. Be careful, Westmore."

"How ambiguous."

"We have to be. God works in fucked up ways. It's the only way because you and your kind can't understand. All of life is a mystery. We're spirits, Westmore. We live forever."

Westmore stared up into dark. Whenever he tried to focus on this phantom—something surely born of his subconscious mind—a vertigo shifted in his vision. Then he was shuddering—the angel was touching his forehead—the gash. The touch felt hot, itchy.

"Parlor tricks for a simpleton." The voice flowed in the dark. The cigarette tip glowed. Westmore wasn't impressed when he touched his forehead and found it healed. No gash, no cut, no blood. *When I wake up tomorrow, it'll be there. I know it'll be there because I know I cut my head. This is just an hallucination, the D.T.'s or something.*

Now the voice sounded like wind blowing through leaves. "You want to see something, you want to see something?" The angel opened his hand over Westmore's eyes. "Remember that girl you loved so much, the one you never told? Take a look."

Westmore saw her in the dark behind his eyes. She was passed out. Some scuzzy scumbag was fucking her.

In the vision, Westmore could sense the man's aura—the core of his being. He was just using her for a hole to fuck. He didn't care the least about her; he'd gotten her drunk just so he could fuck her, and discarded her feelings.

"You should've told her, Westmore," the angel's voice hissed.

The photographer's own voice sounded like something destroyed. "It wouldn't have mattered."

"Let me tell you something about truth…" Now the angel's words seemed to issue from everywhere but his mouth. "The truth *always* matters…"

Westmore ground his teeth; tears squeezed out of the corners of his eyes.

"And here's the crippled kid's digs now. Look, look…"

An executive office, big desk, plaques and certificates of achievement on the paneled walls. On the desk, a framed picture of a happy family.

"He's what you aren't. A success. A benevolent person. He's what it's all about. You aren't."

Westmore was sinking.

The angel stepped back hastily, as if annoyed. "This is chump change, man. Your life is chump change. I don't know why I bother."

"Why *do* you bother?"

More of the hiss-like whisper. "Because you've got to love everyone. You've got to love everyone the way Jesus did. Anything else makes no sense. You're an asshole, but I love you. You're all assholes. A lot of us were really pissed off about your race. A lot of us got thrown out."

"What about you? Did you get thrown out?"

"No. I live to love and serve the Lord on High. I am His unworthy servant forever."

The words beat gently in the air, like small birds flying.

"Because God was right." Again, the angel pointed to his head. "It's what's in here—" and touched his chest—"and what's in here—" then pointed to the windows, "and how you use it out there. Life's a gift. Don't fuck it up. You're fucking it up."

Westmore listened to the ticking clock, staring at the shadow.

The angel flicked the cigarette away, to the tile before the French doors. "It's not possible for you to understand—your brains aren't big enough." He kept pointing to his own head, jabbing a finger. "You can't...cogitate. You cannot...reckon. You do not have the capability of comprehending, man. So that's why we whisper to you in time-held secrets. That's why we unfold as myths and fables. That's why Moses parted the Red Sea. That's why when Jesus said 'Lazarus, come out,' Lazarus came out. It's parlor tricks. You can't understand the whole picture, none of your kind can. God gave you paradise, God gave you perfection and bliss, and you still turned your back on Him. You said 'Fuck you,' to God. You willingly chose error and sin over God's perfect gift. 'You closed the door in My face, so I'm gonna close ALL the doors in your face— all but one. I still love all you assholes, so I'm gonna leave you the option of salvation. I'll tell you what you have to do to do get. But that's it. From here on you're on your own.' You people all chose the wrong road, so now you gotta drive on it, and during the drive you're gonna have to deal with all the things God wanted to protect you from: war, hatred, disease, poverty, failure—ALL that shit. It's no cakewalk. Satan's owned the title-deed to the world since Eve bit the apple and Adam put his fuckin' fig leaf on in shame."

Westmore laughed.

"Come on man. You don't mean that all that biblical shit literally happened? I always thought they were just allegories, sort of like fables."

"Belief is a powerful thing. It shapes the past as well as the future. Once a thing is done and thousands of years have passed, who is to say the manner in which it came to pass? History is what we believe it to be just as God and heaven are what you believe them to be, well, to a point. God does have a definite nature. It's his appearance that changes. Your faith shapes it. There are many different heavens just as there are many different hells and many different types of angels. If you were a Buddhist I may have appeared to you as a lotus blossom."

"Why not as Buddha himself?"

"It's within my power but beyond my authority. That would be akin to appearing to you as Jesus Christ. I'd wind up in Hell myself for that."

"So there are different gods as well?"

"No, only one, but he can take many forms. It all depends on your belief."

"I don't get it."

"Fortunately it's not really necessary that you do. You're not *capable* of getting it."

Westmore's thoughts dripped like blood. He felt becloaked in darkness.

Then the angel said, "Heavy shit's going down in this house. That's why I'm here."

"What kind of heavy shit?"

"An aggrandized affront. Systematized evil. It's a by-product of your fucked up society. The only true society is the society of God."

"I don't know what you're talking about," Westmore grated.

"Of course you don't, because you're too stupid. We work in secrets. Someone has to know. That's why I'm here. Farringworth is an adherent, a living symbol of the corrosion of mankind. He wants to *argue* with God. He thinks that if he pisses God off so completely and precisely, then God'll show Himself." A chuckle like crumbling rocks. "Let me tell you something, Westmore. God's already pissed off. He has been for five thousand years, and He's sick to the nucleus of His soul. He's not going to show Himself—you're not worth His time. God's gone. He's fuckin' busy, man. He gave you a chance. Take it."

Farringworth, the photographer thought. *What did he say? Systematized evil?* Was the angel deliberately being obscure?

"Some things you just gotta find out for yourself," the angel said.

"What *about* Farringworth?" Westmore nearly pleaded. "You're confusing me. I don't know what you mean."

Did the shadowed outline look more grainy?

"Check it out."

"Why are you telling me this?" Westmore asked next.

A floating laugh. "I'm just the messenger. Mine is not to wonder why. God wants me to come to you so I come to you. Yeah, God works in fucked up ways—He sure as shit does 'cos that's the only way you have even the most irreducible chance of getting the big picture."

Westmore's eyes felt propped open by hooks.

The angel was dissolving. "I have to go now, but before I do, I'm going to tell you something. Do you want to hear it?"

Westmore gulped, nodded.

"It's a secret."

"Tell me."

The angel was discomposing in the dark. "If you take the impetus behind the desire to be good, and the impetus behind the desire to be evil—if you put them both together and look at them very closely...you'll see."

"See what?" Westmore croaked.

"They're the same."

The angel was gone.

(VI)

Two men in a room. Night. Quiet.

"The hydrocephalic died," Michaels said. "And the priest had a heart attack."

"Take care of it."

"I already have."

Farringworth sat in a robe of scarlet satin, sipping with little interest from a glass filled with Montrachet 1918. His gaze alternated from the computer monitor to the great bow window, which framed the darkness, tinged in moonlight. Another of his speculative moods, pondering. Michaels knew it was his master's way of dealing with his despair.

"Further appropriations shouldn't be difficult."

"No, they won't be. They're being pursued as we speak," Michaels assured.

Farringworth had the volume turned down on the monitor; he was gloomily watching a variety of clips. First, Betty, stumps reeling in orgasmic jubilation as a Unitarian minister fastidiously fucked her. Next clip: the program director for the United Way, slavering as he performed cunnilingus on an eighteen-year-old girl with Downs' Syndrome, prognathism and cutaneous facial horns. Next clip: two deacons from the Baton Rogue Church of Christ, masturbating rabidly into the face of a woman with a congenital sternal and a genetic defect known as coalition of the bowel. She'd been born with no exterior rectal vent; instead the bowel emptied into the vaginal canal. The camera zoomed closer to her splayed legs as if on cue, as she, in less technical terminology, took a giant spectacular shit from her cunt.

"You're definitely getting your investment's worth from the Metopronil. They *want* to do it. Anything, with anyone, for sexual release," Michaels observed.

But Farrington seemed bored, or forlorn.

He switched to the next scenario, the live camera in the Angels' room. Both monsters slept serenely, entwined in each other's arms amid shining white sheets.

So that's it, Michaels thought. He should've known.

"I'll have them one day," Michaels," the billionaire said very softly. "They'll love me one day."

"I'm sure they will," the attendant replied for lack of anything else, but he was thinking, *Yeah, and I'm sure God will be stopping in any time now.*

He's insane.

Michaels was startled by his employer's next sudden gesture. Just as the attendant had finished the sarcastic thought, Farringworth looked up at him with something like a reproving glare. But a moment later, his eyes went sad again and returned to the monitor.

"And what about our two guests?"

Michaels hated to be the bringer of bad news, but he still wasn't worried. "We've already contained Bryant. And, well, don't be alarmed, but—"

Farringworth snapped up another sharp glare.

"—The photographer isn't in his room."

"What?"

"You needn't worry. He's probably stumbling around here drunk. My men aren't back yet from disposing of the priest and the child."

It was Michaels' good fortune that looks couldn't kill.

"We'll find the photographer," the Englander assured. "It's impossible for him to get out of the house."

Farringworth's reply sounded like the worst omen. "It better be."

(VII)

Westmore regained consciousness, oblivious. He lay beneath the table, cloaked in darkness, and at first he could remember nothing. His thoughts ticked along with the clock.

An angel, huh?

Surely, he'd passed out from too much scotch, and dreamed the whole thing, but even in the dim moonlight streaming in through the French doors, he could see the bloodstains on his shirt. He'd hit his head against the edge of the armoire, but his head didn't hurt at all. He felt at the wound and there was no wound.

He dragged himself up, pressed the stem of his watch to light the dial. 4:12 a.m. He fingered his top pocket for a cigarette yet found the pack empty. *Maybe the angel ripped off all my cigarettes,* he thought as a joke. But he wasn't laughing. On the immaculate tile flooring before the door, a cigarette butt lay, as if flicked there.

What could he tell Bryant? Nothing. *I had a hallucination, I had a hallucination. I was drunk. I hit my head but the cut must be on my scalp; that's where the blood came from. And it was me who flicked the cigarette butt on the floor. It was not a foul-mouthed, wingless angel in a black t-shirt. It was not.*

He felt sick now but not from drinking. It was his heart that felt sick. It was the vibes. He was not acting on cryptic messages from a hallucination of an angel, but he felt he had to do something.

Check it out, the mirage had said.

Westmore took a deep breath, took a few steps to see if he could walk, then felt his way out of the room toward the stairs. Words like leaves blowing through gutters haunted him up to the second floor landing: *An aggrandized affront. Systematized evil.* And: *Heavy shit's going down in this house.*

"Forget it, forget it," he mumbled to himself. "Just...find Bryant."

He didn't even know exactly why he needed to find Bryant. It was just an inclination, perhaps one rooted in uselessness. Westmore felt perplexed and useless. And scared. He didn't really trust anybody on the face of the earth—he'd spent his entire life trusting the untrustworthy, a fool—and he didn't even now at this point if he trusted himself, especially shit-faced.

But he trusted his inclinations. He trusted the vibes.

"Bryant?" he kept his voice down when he opened his partner's bedroom door and looked in.

The room was a shambles. Bryant wasn't there.

(VIII)

"You weren't easy to subdue."

The accent rang: British. Bryant's head rang, too. Felt like somebody hit him in the head with a hammer. *Damn...* Acidic splotches of memory—like bile in someone's throat—kept slipping up. *Several men,* he recalled. They'd come into his room when he was asleep.

"You put up quite a fight," Michaels said, looking down.

Bryant remembered more. Thrashing. After the fight, the room was wrecked and Bryant was straitjacketed.

And here he sat, unable to move against the canvas constraints, in another room. Not the bedroom he'd been shown.

It was a horror show. It was a room of freaks. Bryant was speechless, at first not even believing his own eyes.

A bright room, with bright overhead lights. Were multiple cameras mounted in the ceiling? He thought so. And there were...things. Pale, quivering things...

"This is where we do it," Michaels said. "It is from this room that Mr. Farringworth puts forth his challenge to God."

Bryant thought he might throw up when he took his first look. There were several beds arranged about the room, and on each one lay some twisted, naked form—some biological accident. It took him a moment to actually realize that the forms were human.

"We house monsters here, and this is our work room, so to speak. But we care for them quite well—Mr. Farringworth actually loves them, in his own way. He's fascinated by the imperfect, and the derivatives of that imperfection."

One contorted, slobbering woman was being wheeled out now in a wheelchair. Did she have horns or spikes coming out of her face? Her head looked squashed. On another bed a deathly thin man twitched. He suffered from muscular and adipose atrophy—a living skeleton. A raging erection bobbed as he twitched. Eventually, men in suits gently put the tragedy in a chair and wheeled him out.

"What in God's name are you doing?" Bryant finally got it out.

"In God's name—yes. How ironic. You'll understand in due time. Oh, and I hate to tell you this, but..." Michaels smiled, then held up a piece of paper that Bryant recognized at once as a blueline, an editor's proof. "Can you read this? Is your vision blurred from the skirmish?"

"What is it?

"Your obituary."

Bryant's heart thudded as he read.

—The editors and staff are saddened to report the deaths of finance journalist James Bryant and photographer Richard Westmore, both well known in the field.

Bryant and Westmore worked together often, interviewing some of the most successful financiers in the world. They were both killed Wednesday in a taxicab accident near Metro Detroit airport. They will be sorely missed. Services will be held at—

This is crazy, Bryant thought. "My boss knows we're here, you idiot. I talked to him yesterday on my cell phone—from this house."

"Mr. Bryant—" Michaels wagged the sheet of paper. "This is a blueline for the next issue of *Blue Chip,* the magazine you and Westmore work for. This was all planned well in advance, and I'm happy to say that your boss was all too cooperative."

Bryant struggled against the restraints, swamped in confusion. "He's agreed to run an obituary when he knows we're alive?"

"Oh, yes. In the past, wisdom has been power, but today it's money. And Mr. Farringworth paid of a lot of that to your boss to go along with this ruse. The bodies, of course, were burned beyond recognition, and further palms were greased, so to speak, to insure the proper placement of falsified DNA reports. To the rest of the world, Mr. Bryant, you're dead."

"So...what? Now you're gonna kill me? That's ridiculous. You don't know me, I'm no threat to you, and neither is Westmore!"

Michaels didn't move, just kept looking down, hands behind his back. "No, no, we're not going to kill you. We *want* you. You will be the chronicler, Westmore the photographer."

"Chronicler for what! Photographer for what!"

"For Mr. Farringworth's life, of course. And his

work—or I should say, not his financial pursuits—that's just his hobby. His real work, the work he does here. You and Westmore will never leave this house again. You will write Farringworth's biography and philosophical study, and your colleague will compile the photographic archive."

"Of what?"

"Mr. Farringworth's endeavors, to be released long in the future, when he dies. It will be the mark he leaves on the rampart of history. You needn't worry. All your needs will be taken care of—" Michaels turned at the sound of a door clicking open. New tragedies were being wheeled in to the bed: a seven-foot-tall woman with acromegaly, a two-headed conjoined twin, a Thalidomide woman...

"—Including your sexual needs."

Gagging and other strange noises came from the beds. Several men were led into the room, faces flushed, a rage in their eyes, erections gorged. They looked crazed with lust. They climbed onto the beds and began to...

Aw, Christ, Bryant thought, stomach tensing. But then his brows shot up when Michaels came around behind. The British attendant was unbuckling the straitjacket.

"You're thinking that I'm either very confident about my abilities to defend myself," Michaels began, "or I'm very stupid. I'm taking this straitjacket off and giving you full reign of the house, to move about as you please. And when you find your friend Westmore, please advise him of the current situation."

The jacket's canvas straps came loose. Bryant–a very large man–shrugged it off, stood up, and turned, preparing to destroy Michaels in place.

"Here's why you *won't* lay a hand on me," and then the Englander handed Bryant a stack of photos. Bryant flipped through them, getting sicker with each snapshot. *All my relatives,* he realized. Candid outdoor shots–as if taken secretly from a car–showed him his parents, his Uncle Eddie and Aunt Amelia, his sister, his nephew and niece.

"So you can see, Mr. Bryant. If you fail to cooperate with us in any way, or if I don't walk out that door in a few minutes, all of your loved ones will be killed. We'll kill them slowly and gruelingly. We'll bring them here to do it. We'll make you watch."

Bryant's shoulders drooped. He'd never felt more defeated in his life.

"And you're overlooking the best part. Consider your new alliance with us as a privilege, an adventure, not imprisonment. You see, if you're lucky, perhaps Farringworth will succeed." Michaels' grin seemed to hover in the harsh lights. "You may get to meet God."

Bryant sat back down. "You're insane."

"No. I'm not. But Farringworth is."

(IX)

Later.

The horror had become an accretion. This was Bryant's research, watching this. *This is what I have to write about,* he thought. He tried to focus, to be objective, however impossible that prospect seemed. "How can they? How can they have sex with these freaks?"

Micheals smiled wide.

"Drugs, Mr. Bryant. The most potent aphrodisiac

ever produced. It's called Metopronil and the pharmaceutical company that Mr. Farringworth now owns developed it. It increases activity in the limbic system of the brain, most specifically in the amygdala, the rage center or visceral brain, which also controls sexual impulses. It raises serotonin levels dramatically causing violent sexual impulses, actually altering normal brain activity giving the subject the brain patterns of a serial rapist. In fact, it was by studying the brain activity of rapists, signature sex killers, and other sexual predators that we were able to develop the drug. "

"That is truly fucking sick. So all those trucks we kept seeing coming back and forth. They were dropping off more of this stuff?"

"Some of them were. Some of them carried more of our guests. Would you like to see the rest of our home?"

Michaels began walking across the room towards a door on the far end of the hall. Bryant had no choice but to follow. He didn't want to spend another second in that room.

"This way to our guest suites. This is where we place our new arrivals until they learn to cooperate."

They walked down a hall lined with locked doors before entering a small room that looked like the security booth of a major casino. Video monitors dominated one entire wall with DVD recorders documenting every thrust and moan. Michaels sat down before the bank of monitors and took hold of the tiny red joystick that controlled each camera. The largest screen showed a diminutive Asian man with a shaved head sitting naked in the lotus position. His eyes were closed and he appeared to be deep in meditation but his face was anything but serene.

Sweat bulleted down his face and his jaw muscles clenched and unclenched. From between his crossed legs an erection was clearly visible. He'd obviously been injected with the Metopronil, but he was fighting it. The effort seemed to be draining every ounce of his strength. Bryant could see him tremble and shiver as if stricken by fever. Across from him lay a woman whose limbs were twisted and bowed like curly fries. She too was nude and her eyes gleamed with want. They both sat silently in the little room, delirious with desire.

"That's Sato Masaaki. He's a Zen Buddhist monk and founder of the Temple of Enlightenment, with followers all over the world. He has enough Metopronil surging through his veins to start an orgy in a Mormon Temple. He'll break soon."

"How long has he been like that?"

"Mr. Masaaki has been with us for a little over three weeks."

"Trapped in that room? With that freak? Doped up on aphrodisiacs? My God."

"Yes, poor Sharon is no doubt suffering more than he is. She doesn't have his will-power and the hypo-osteopesis which has curled her bones has left her incapable of self-satisfaction."

"You mean you doped her up too?"

"But, of course. If it was just his own suffering he had to deal with then that wouldn't be as much fun. Now though, his obstinacy is causing someone else to suffer as well. She can't speak, but he can still hear her whimper and groan. He can imagine how difficult it must be for her to cope with the drug because of his own painful struggle to resist it. It's a hundred times worse than heroin withdrawal. Reproduction is one of your most primary biological drives. Every cell in your body has the desire to reproduce. By resisting the drug he is at battle with every fiber of his being just as she is. And, being a Buddhist, he has no choice but to empathize with her. In his mind she and he are one, just as he is one with all things. Her suffering is his own, magnifying his pain twofold."

"But why? Why are you doing all this?" Bryant asked, eyes wide in utter disbelief. In his wildest dreams he could never have imagined anything so sadistic.

"Just as Mr. Farringworth has said. In order to enrage an omni-benevolent and very vain and jealous deity. To make him angry enough to reveal himself."

"But that's insane! That's never going to happen."

"Perhaps not, but if anything will do it, it would be breaking that monk. He's the most pious human being we've yet to come across. All the rest of them had sins on their hearts, hidden lusts that the drug could bring to the surface. But not this one. He's as pure as the driven snow in his heart and his soul. Getting him to fuck that crippled freak until she cries out for Jesus, or Buddha, or whoever, would be our greatest achievement yet. Ah, here's Minister Farrahd."

"Minister Far—? You mean the Black Muslim leader!"

"One in the same. It will be interesting to see how he enjoys our angels."

"Angels?"

"Just look."

Michaels pointed to another screen. He swiveled the joystick until the camera landed on the two pale willowy twins. They were so tall that their heads nearly scraped the ceiling. Their ghostly white skin glowed

with an unearthly luminescence beneath the bright fluo-
rescent overhead lights. Waist-length platinum hair
swirled around the two gigantic twins as if animated as
they approached the bald black man whose cock was
already urgently erect and glistening with pre-cum. His
eyes were wild and he was sweating and twitching with
the effects of the Metopronil.

Bryant couldn't take his eyes off the twins, the
angels. With an audible gasp, he took notice of their
confusion of oversized primary and secondary sex
organs. He'd never seen more beautiful breasts and their
cocks were a porn director's dream, so long and heavy
that even fully erect they were too weighty to stand
upright but rather leaned to the left or right swaying like
divining rods. Beneath their penises, where testicles
should have been, swollen pink labia blossomed like
roses around yawning vaginal pits, wide enough to fit
two fists and probably the forearms as well up to the
elbows.

"Who the hell have they been fucking?" Bryant
wondered, then he answered his own question when the
two elegant creatures turned and kissed each other, their
tongues lashing out like adders, striking and con-
stricting.

Their eyes gleamed with an animalistic lust that was
truly frightening on creatures so huge. The two hermaphrodites' massive penises would easily disembowel
the helpless Minister. He could see why they called
them the angels. They could have been descendants of
the Nephilim, the gigantic hybrids of humans and angels
that were said to have once walked the earth before the
great flood. Bryant found himself both sickened and
intrigued.

"Do you dope up all the freaks too?" Bryant asked, staring in awe at the angel's tremendous sex organs.

"Only sometimes, when it's necessary. Most often it isn't. They're usually quite delighted with all the attention they receive from our guests. Not these two though. They aren't very receptive to others."

The minister knelt naked on the floor weeping as he stared up at the two pale devils standing above him. He turned to the east and prayed for Allah to rescue him from temptation. Still, his erection bulged shamelessly as he took in the two beautiful titans.

"The Minister believes all white men are the devil, mutants created by a mad scientist named Dr. Yacub some five thousand years ago in order to oppress the black race. He preaches separatism and vengeance, hates all things Caucasian. He also believes homosexuality to be a sin. How wonderful will it be when the Metopronil cracks his resolve and he submits himself to sodomy at the hands of two albino hermaphrodites? He doesn't even realize he's been drugged. We put it in his food and in his water. He'll think the weakness lies within himself. In all likelihood he'll kill himself once we tell him that his sins have been recorded and aired all over the country. That is, if the twins don't kill him first." Michaels grinned sadistically as the minister rose from his knees, sporting the largest erection of his life, and advanced on the two gigantic hermaphrodites who stood regarding him with curious detachment.

Bryant felt some part of himself wilt when the proud minister dropped to his knees and began licking and sucking on one impossibly long albescent cock. Slurping on it like some half-starved infant on its mother's tit. Bryant had no real love for the Black

Islamic tradition in America. He had never condoned its racist politics and practices. He was more than familiar with the hate that hate made. He too had often been the victim of prejudice, but he believed that the answer was not to meet prejudice with more prejudice. That only perpetuated the cycle. He believed that you used love to combat hatred. Still, he could not deny the unifying effect the Minister had on the black community. He had a way of galvanizing people with his fiery speeches, making them listen and want to change themselves for the better. Some part of him had always admired the man's efforts. He'd given millions of black men something to believe in and, love him or hate him, he had a way of earning your respect. But no one would respect him now. After this tape hit the streets, The Brotherhood of Islam would be dead.

"Does that drug always work? I mean does it have the same effect on everyone?"

"Well, nothing is 100% effective, although on males it seems to be. Women seem to be better able to resist it. I guess if Farringworth could develop an aphrodisiac that was absolutely effective on women he wouldn't need to find God. He'd *be* God. It doesn't seem to work on the twins most of the time either. It could be all the female hormones. And when it does work, it wears off quickly. We got lucky today. Either that or they really like that minister."

One of the twins was forcing his fifteen-inch phallus into the minister's rectum while the other fed his cock down Farrahd's throat. He looked like a pig on a spit. Their thrusts became more forceful, violently raping the Minister's esophagus and asshole. Soon Farrahd was bleeding from both ends. One of the twins withdrew his cock from Farrahd throat as the other thrust the last seven inches of his erection deep into the minister's bowels, causing an explosion of gore to erupt from the man's mouth and splatter onto the floor. Once he'd finished heaving up the larger portion of his internal organs, the other twin once more slid his rigid flesh down the man's esophagus, fucking his dying corpse until they roared with orgasm and semen began streaming from the minister's mouth and nose along with the blood. Bryant turned his head. He felt ill.

"I don't know if the drug really works on them at all or if they just get in sadistic moods and decide it might be fun to fuck someone to death."

Bryant's stomach lurched.

"What happens to the women who are immune?"

"That's the beautiful thing about women, they don't really need to consent to sex for it to happen."

Micheals pointed to the screen above them and turned his joystick so that the camera zoomed in. The horror just never seemed to stop.

"The skinny man with olive skin is Yogi Ramakenada. The drug is having a wonderful effect on him. The emaciated scarecrow he's about to ravage wasn't so lucky. She's pretty much immune to the stuff. Her name is Leticia Sum— uh, no need for you to know her last name. She has Malign Hypermetabolism which means that her body does not store fat and anything she consumes runs through her in minutes. Leticia has to eat every 30 minutes or she'll die. She consumes 125% of her body weight everyday. Her sex drive is non-existent. The only drive she has is hunger. Ever watch preying mantises mate?"

Michaels was grinning again.

Behind him, on the screen, a Hindu man in an orange robe was biting through his bottom lip and frothing at the mouth as he fought to subdue the riot of want rampaging through his nervous system. An impossibly gaunt woman danced before him, bending over and grabbing her ankles in an effort to entice him into mounting her shriveled buttocks, which was little more than a coccyx with pale mottled skin draped over it.

"It looks to me like the drug is working. Look at how she's flirting with him."

"She's luring prey." Micheals replied. "Just watch. See, the Metopronil has already broken his will. The Yogi is dying for a piece of her emaciated arse. He's a Hindu master who can withstand depths of pain you could scarcely imagine without batting an eye. He can hold his breath underwater for nearly an hour and squeeze his narrow frame into a box no bigger than a milk crate. But in seconds he'll forget all about Dharma and life and truth and he'll fuck that skeletal witch until she snaps like a twig or until she gets hungry again and starts eating him alive. See, like most who suffer from her particular disability, Leticia's a cannibal."

The Yogi launched across the room almost tackling the woman as he tore his robes aside and his engorged penis bounced free. He mounted her in the position customary to mammals and began hammering into her so hard you could hear pelvic bone striking pelvic bone, echoing like swordplay in the tiny room.

"Yes. Yessssss." Leticia moaned and her eyes were glassy with hunger. She pulled the yogi down onto the bed with her and spun around so that they were now in the missionary position without breaking contact for a second. The yogi was thrusting as if trying to enter her womb, testicles and all. Leticia reached out and encircled his neck with her cadaverous arms, pulling him closer. As he buried his head into her shoulder, bearing down so that he could thrust still harder, Leticia opened her jaws revealing a charnel pit of bloodstained teeth that had been filed to sharp points. Her mouth closed on his throat and she began ripping and tearing out huge chunks, immediately swallowing them. The Yogi didn't miss a single thrust. Even as he screamed he continued to pound in and out of the withered starveling while she ripped more meat out of his neck. Bryant shook his head in wonder as she reached his cervical vertebrae and began trying to chew through that as well.

Like the monkey with his hand in the cookie jar, the yogi refused to withdraw from her loins even to save his own life. Despite the unimaginable pain, they both appeared to be in ecstasy.

"I need to find my photographer. Would you take me back to my room?"

"Of course. You will be provided with copies of all of these tapes and you will bear witness to all the events up to and including the day Mr. Farrington achieves his end."

"Yeah…uh…sure. Look, this is a lot of shit to digest. Let me talk to Westmore and we'll get back to you about all of this."

"That's fine. You can talk it over amongst yourselves, but as I said. You really have no choice in the matter. You are either one of us…" The smile drained from Michaels face. Only then did Bryant notice how cruel the man's face truly was. Hard angular features with dark eyes sunk deep into his head like Lurch from the old Adam's Family T.V. show. Michaels gestured toward the screen where

Minister Farrahd's corpse was still impaled on the monstrous cocks of the twin hermaphrodites then to the one where the hyperphagic cannibal was busily chewing off the head of Yogi Ramakenada. She had already eaten away most of his face yet his ass continued to rise up and down, thrusting deep into her with psychotic enthusiasm. The smile slithered back onto Michael's face. "...Or you are one of them."

(X)

Bryant's chocolate brown complexion had turned completely gray. He stumbled into the room swaying unsteadily as if he were about to feint dead away. His brow rose. Did he hear something–a tick?–from the closet. He swung the door open, and Westmore about screamed.

"Finally found you. They don't even care that you're trying to hide. You can't get out. No one can."

Westmore was holding a cell phone and trying vainly to get an outside line.

"Don't even bother with the cell. They took the batteries out. We're completely cut off from the outside world. We're both fucking dead men."

"Dead men? What are you talking about? What the fuck happened to you, man?"

"We're in trouble, Richard. I mean we are completely fucked." His hand trembled as he snatched the snifter of brandy from Westmore's hand and downed it in two quick gulps.

"Okay, man, now you're freaking me out. What's going on?"

Bryant began explaining their predicament as best he could, stopping frequently to refill his glass and down more of the fiery brandy. He relayed the story of how they had been tricked up here to act as Farrington's biographers, even telling him about the fake obituary. He then told him about the monk he'd seen locked up in the room with the contorted freak doped up on some kind of steroidal aphrodisiac. Soon they were passing the bottle back and forth and drinking straight from the neck like two hobos.

"You have got to be fucking kidding me? He's the guy who's been putting all that scandalous sex stuff out on the internet? Farringworth? He's the one who scandalized the Southern Baptist Ministries with that tape of Reverend Willis getting fist-fucked by the werewolf bitch?"

"It was a girl with hypertrichosis and yes, Farringworth was behind it. And if we don't help him out then we'll be the next ones to be fed to his freaks."

"So that's what the angel meant about systemized evil."

"The angel? You've seen the angels?" The image of Minister Farrahd being run through by the twin's yard-long penises was still vivid in his mind. He could still see the ecstasy in the man's eyes as his internal organs were ruptured and displaced by their frenetic thrusts.

"Just one." Westmore replied, bringing Bryant back from his grim reverie. "He appeared in my bedroom and told me that God had sent me to stop Farringworth."

Westmore looked down at his feet, obviously embarrassed by this admission.

"Okay, what the hell are you talking about?"

"I'm talking about an angel and no I'm not drunk,

well, not much. He was standing right there at the foot of the bed, and then I saw him downstairs. He looked sort of like Bob Dylan but with darker hair. What angels are you talking about?"

Bryant relayed the story of the acromegalic hermaphrodites sodomizing Minister Farrahd.

"Holy shit. You mean that headline hogging Black Muslim guy? What a trip. You think those were the angels that Farringworth was going on about when we saw him on the stairs?"

"It sure as hell wasn't any nicotine addicted Bob Dylan look-alike."

"So what do we do?"

"What choice do we have? We go along with it until we can figure out a way to get out of here."

"But...but what if it works?"

"What?"

"I know it's crazy, but if God sent one of his angels down to warn us about this shit then maybe Farringworth is on to something. I mean what if he gets that little monk to crack and succeeds in bringing God down from heaven? What if he succeeds in becoming a god himself? Is that the type of guy you want to see with infinite power? Even if this is all bullshit, just think of how many lives he's damaging with his crusade against religious leaders? How many people around the world look up to the people this madman has got doped up in little rooms getting fucked half to death by his monstrosities?"

"So what are you saying?"

"I'm saying we can't just escape. We need to try to stop him."

Westmore nodded grimly. "But how? We can't get out."

"Not without keys. We'll just have to find some, and we'll probably have to kill some people in the process."

"Great," Westmore said, but he knew it was true. "If we don't take a chance, we'll never get out of this madhouse."

"Right, so let's not fuck around. Let's burn the house down."

"A place like this?" Westmore objected. "It ain't gonna be easy to burn down. Look." Westmore pointed upward, to the sprinkler nozzles in the ceiling.

"Find a way to disable them, turn the water off or something. That'll be your job."

"My job, huh?" Westmore lit a cigarette, frowning. "So what's *your* job?"

"My job is to find Farringworth and kill him," Bryant said. "And I'll whack that British guy, too. I don't like his face."

"Cool," Westmore approved.

"We can either be prisoners here for the rest of our lives, or we go for broke. Get those sprinklers turned off and start torching the house. If we're lucky, we'll be able to get somebody's keys and maybe even get some of those fucked-up people out in the confusion."

"Yeah, and what if we're *not* lucky?" Westmore couldn't resist asking.

"Then we both die. But I'm willing to take the chance." Bryant looked around. "This place should not be allowed to exist."

(XI)

Sharon shuddered in the crush of confusion and unknown sensation. She wasn't really smart enough to think, *What's happening to me?* But at least in some circuitous way, she was aware of the inclination. The yawning gulf between her legs seemed aflame in urgency; her clitoris was an ember that needed to be stoked. Her condition, regrettably, would not allow her to touch herself in any masturbatory manner, so she kind of squirmed with her bowed legs together, rocking back and forth, which caused a blaze of pleasure in her sex. She needed that blaze to explode but she also weakly realized that that would never happen if the little bald man refused to touch her. She wanted him to touch her the way Louie did back at the care center. If she had the mental capacity to put her rage of desires into words it would be that she wanted the bald man to ball her to kingdom come, to pound her like sod, to just purely and simply fuck the living shit out of her. She didn't care about anything else, couldn't care. Sharon was insane now, with unmitigated lust.

She shimmied in the bed, the overhead lights blaring in her malformed face. She was a heaving, flesh-colored pretzel, her curled limbs and runneled rib cage quivering. Meanwhile, the bald man–the monk–looked insane too, the unrelieved cock drooling. If anything, Sato Masaaki was now something more than human, an embodiment of the power of will over nature. Yes, his own will was stronger than anything else on earth at that moment, as he measured his agony along with Sharon's and still was able to say no. No to the physical. No to pleasure. No to lust.

Yes to the power of spirit.

Then a technician walked in and injected him with more Metopronil...

(XII)

Westmore watched the Englander leave the room and disappear down the hall. Bryant had suggested they split up, their goal being to find a weakness, the one bad link in the chain to exploit. Sure, the house was a fortress, but there had to be a way out. Westmore was determined to find it, but...

The vibes again.

He just had a bad feeling.

I don't think I'm gonna get out of here alive...

He didn't know if he even wanted to live. After what Bryant had told him, and after what he'd seen in some of those rooms? *The angel was right. There's some heavy shit going down in this house.* He'd only taken a few nauseated peeks when he'd snuck down one of the upstairs hallways. Religious figureheads being chemically forced to rape invalids and deformees. Who could think of something like that? Who could possibly *want* such a thing?

Farringworth, obviously. Truly a madman, but then the most unpleasant notion of all struck Westmore.

What if he's NOT a madman? What if he's for real?

Westmore was no crusader. He was a busted, forlorn drunk. But he had to do something.

Good God almighty, he thought when he slipped into the room that the Brit had just left. A control room sort of place, full of video screens. At first he thought it was a security room, but he quickly noted that the monitors weren't hooked up to any security cameras. They were recording the sexual atrocities taking place in the rooms on the other wing.

Each monitor was an eye looking into hell.

Westmore threw up in the corner; he almost collapsed. *No, no, no,* he thought. *This ain't makin' it. Bryant's right. We have to burn this place to the fucking ground and take Farringworth OUT...*

Westmore couldn't look at the screens anymore but he did notice a panel of buttons. He pressed a button that said GARAGE, and a monitor switched to that: a garage facility somewhere on the premise. A Rolls Royce White Shadow, several BMW's, and a couple of those pharmaceutical vans. Another button read UTILITY. Westmore pressed it, looked.

Then he had the answer.

He left swiftly, and it's a good thing he did. Otherwise he might have seen what was going on in the room with the bald monk.

(XIII)

Just when Sato Masaaki had reached the ultimate level of spiritual perfection–the point where the power of his will defeated natural drive—the next dose of Metopronil kicked in. It seemed like a dream, or a vision from some very high place. Was someone with him? A barely embodied light seemed to whisper to him, grinning.

Then this being, this entity or whatever it was–touched him, not so much physically but in some discorporate way, and then all the evil of history poured through his mind like a black waterfall. From the beginning of time, he saw it all, the endless dark kaleidoscope that was true human nature. Lust, greed, gluttony, wrath. Hatred.

Yes, he saw it all, the true realities, the true components of mankind. But if those were the *true* components, where did that leave his own ideologies? Did that mean his own truths were really lies?

Sato Masaaki no longer cared. His resolve collapsed like a demolitioned building.

He would spend the next several hours fucking the hypo-osteopetic girl to pulp.

(XIV)

This is too easy, Westmore thought. He snuck about the house for over an hour before he actually found the utility room he'd seen on the monitor upstairs. The mansion was labyrinthine, under-rooted by a basement level running with narrow corridors. Eventually he found one door that read GARAGE and was not surprised to find the steel-framed door deadbolted. *I'd need a fuckin' howitzer to get through that.* But then he found the utility room and almost did a rebel yell.

It was right there staring him in the face. A red-painted valve and a plaque that read MAIN WATER SHUT-OFF. *Yeah, this is too fuckin' easy,* he thought again and lit a cigarette. There was even a convenient fire ax in a glass case right by the door. He smashed the glass, removed the ax, and hefted it in his hands. *If Bryant doesn't get Farringworth and the Brit, I will.*

They'll have the keys to that exit door, he knew. *I'll cut both their fuckin' heads off if I have to, but I'll GET those keys.*

The plan was simple and the only one available. In a moment he'd close the valve to the central water main, which would render the sprinkler system useless. Then he'd start to light the place up. Sure, it was risky, and, sure, the chances of escaping were ultra-slim, but after seeing what was going on here? Westmore agreed wholeheartedly with his associate. They couldn't let this go on. A place like this should never exist, and Westmore would be pleased to help remove it from the face of the earth.

No time like the present, he thought.

He reached for the main water valve, was about to grab it with his hands, but—

Two *other* hands grabbed him.

Westmore didn't have time to shout. He was thrown to the other side of the room as if he were a bag of packing curls. Above him, the deformed shadow loomed.

At first, Westmore thought his attacker must be the Devil himself, but if anything it was uglier. It was Billy Meyers: huge, naked, sweat dripping off his misshapen muscles. Jacked up on madness and jacked up even more on Metopronil, his warped eyes beamed. His elephantine penis was gorged as if fit to burst, big as a tube of chalk with veins stout as I.V. line. The extra teeth crammed in the grin looked caked with shit. The neurofibromotosis had turned his head into a turret-like growth with eyes, one blue, one green. He reached down with his elbowless left arm and pawed Westmore's face, leaving a smear of excrement.

Billy's intentions were all-too-clear. He was all over Westmore, the gorged cock thumping against the photographer's chest, testicles heavy as plums. The thing continued to paw Westmore's face, dry-humping him. But Westmore was pinned to the floor by the other hand, which easily girded his throat; the grip felt like a slowly tightening clamp.

Not like this, not like this, Westmore pleaded, but who was he pleading to? God? The angel? Or his own bad karma? He knew he was going to die, and he didn't really even care. He just didn't want to die like *this.* Sex-fodder for a genuine monster.

Now Westmore couldn't breathe. His vision dimmed. This was it, this was the end. In a moment he'd be dead...

He heard a *thwack!* And then a high, whinnying sound that couldn't possibly be human but was nonetheless. The monster rolled off, shuddering, feeling desperately for something at his back. In his last moments, driven more by reflexive instinct than volition, Westmore had managed to grab the fire ax and sink it into the small of Billy's back. The pillars of muscle that were his legs thrashed on the floor. Westmore pulled away, but the malformed hand found his collar and yanked.

Clack, clack, clack!

Billy's double row of teeth snapped, just a half inch away from Westmore's face, then he yanked him closer. Westmore jammed a thumb into the green eye a split second before he would lose chunks of face.

Another whinnying howl, when the photographer dragged the ax out of Billy's back and heaved the blade into the monster's crotch, dividing the balls. Blood poured. Another thwack, and Westmore cut Billy's cock in half. The blood that blew out of the massive erection looked pressurized.

Westmore jumped up, sucked in a deep breath, and drove the ax a final time into Billy's rock-formation-like forehead. Speckles of blood blasted back, dotting Westmore's face.

He leaned back, paralyzed with exhaustion. He looked down at the mess on the floor–the cleaved corpse, the long chunk of severed cock, the pool of blood–and almost passed out. Then he staggered to the water valve and cranked it shut.

He took one last look at Billy's body, then thought, *Fuck this shit, man. I need a drink...* But there was no time for that. A can of cleaning solvent sat on a shelf. He grabbed it, grabbed the ax, and walked out of the room. It was time to start burning this motherfucker down.

(XV)

Bryant hid out a while, ducking back into the monitor room. In truth, he knew neither he nor Westmore stood much of a chance against such odds, but that realization actually revitalized him. When you wrote off your own life, you had nothing to lose. At first, he thought it must be his imagination when he thought he smelled smoke. Then he looked at one of the screens, saw that it had been switched to the utility room, and saw the hacked corpse of the neurofibromotosis victim. It wasn't pretty, but Bryant was amazed. *I don't believe it, he fucking did it, he turned off the water and turned that thing into cold cuts.* He could see the arrow on the water main valve turned to the closed position. He peeked out the door and saw the faintest veil of smoke hanging in the air. Westmore was taking care of the house, now Bryant needed to take care of Farringworth, wherever he was. *Guess I'll just half to go on a tear-ass, kill Farringworth, get his keys, and try to find Westmore and get out.*

Then he thought: *Wait a minute!*

There he was right there.

Bryant caught movement on one the screens. The bald monk was copulating viciously with a defected victim, and sitting in the corner of the same room, watching it all, was Farringworth. The billionaire sat naked and perfectly still, gazing intently at the horror on the bed, and propped upright between his legs was an obese woman with no arms or legs. She was slowly fellating Farringworth.

Bryant remembered the room, it was where he'd been originally taken after they'd straitjacketed him, when Michaels had let him know the full score. The room was just down the hall.

But when he opened the door to leave for that room, Michaels faced him from the doorway, a pistol in his face. Bryant edged back into the room.

"Where is your associate, Mr. Bryant?"

"I got no idea."

"It seems he's running about lighting fires. It's a waste of time, though. This house has a multimillion-dollar sprinkler system."

Don't count on it, Bryant thought.

"I do hope you've been paying attention," the Englander said next.

"To what?"

Michaels pointed to the screen. "To the festivities. The monk broke. His spirit is gone. He's destroying that poor woman. Look."

Bryant didn't look; he'd seen enough. "You really think God's going to show up?"

"Who knows," the response seemed to float in the air.

This was a stalemate. Bryant already knew what he had to do so he didn't deliberate. He simply did it.

He spun, offering the least target space to Michaels, knowing he'd probably be hit. The movement did indeed cause the Englander to fire, then:

Snap!

Clink!

–The small silenced pistol cycled. Bryant was so charged with adrenalin, he didn't feel the pain. The bullet caught him in the right arm, but with his left he clotheslined Michaels. The gun flew out of his hand when he hit the ground, and by the time he regained his senses, Bryant had retrieved it. Now *he* was pointing the gun in *Michaels* face.

"Give me a reason," Bryant said, feeling the British man's pockets. There was nothing, no keys of any kind in any of them. "Every exit door in this place is locked from the inside. Where are the keys?"

Michaels smiled triumphantly. "They're voice-printed. Only my voice and Farringworth's can open them. Look's like you'll have to take me with you, hmm?"

"You're too much of a pain in the ass," Bryant replied. "And you know something? I really don't like your face."

Snap!

Clink!

Bryant put a bullet in the center of Michaels' chest.

I'll get Farringworth to open the door, he resolved. *After I kneecap the son of a bitch.*

He was about to leave when he felt something tugging his pants cuff. It was Michaels, still alive but not for long, blood looping out of the bullet hole that pierced his aorta.

"What do you what?" the journalist asked.

Michaels couldn't answer in voice. His arm slowly rose, his index finger extended. The Englander was pointing at the monitor in Sato Masaaki's room.

All Bryant could do was stare.

It looked like Masaaki's room had filled with light.

(XVI)

Bryant practically trampled the dying manservant as he burst out of the security room and sprinted down the hallway. Outside Masaaki's room the light was eating through the cracks in the doorway, blackening and searing away the paint on the opposite wall. As Bryant reached the door a piercing scream blasted his eardrums and sent shivers rattling up his vertebrae. Someone in that room was in indescribable agony. The smell of burnt hair and flesh came wafting from within, roaring in Bryant's nostrils and churning the bile in his stomach. The journalist paused just beyond the door and leaned against the wall, listening to the shrill cries of pain and struggling to overcome his fear and nausea. He stuck a hand tentatively into the blistering light emanating from the doorway and felt a heat that tightened his skin and opened his sweat glands but thankfully didn't burn.

"Thank heaven for melanin." He thought as he prepared to wrench open the door and empty the gun into Farringworth.

Bryant had never killed anyone. His parents had moved him out of Oakland to Santa Cruz California when he was only six years old to ensure that he'd never have to. Now here he was, crouching in a hallway with a loaded gun about to murder a madman in order to prevent him from becoming God. And if that light was what he feared it was, than he'd be killing the man in full sight of the all-mighty.

"This just can't be happening." Bryant shook his head and chuckled to his self as he looked down at the automatic pistol in his hand.

"What the fuck am I doing here?" A day ago he didn't even believe in God. Now he was about to meet him face to face.

Slowly he turned the doorknob as his heart trip-hammered in his chest and his body trembled as if it had been doused with ice water and plugged into a light socket. Bryant took a deep breath, clicked the 9mm Beretta off safety, and prepared to yank open the door when it exploded from within and a body came crashing through it, landing in the hallway in a steaming heap. Bryant looked down at the man who was covered in blisters and third degree burns, his penis a blackened stump that looked more like a spent match then human flesh. It was Sato Masaaki.

"Evil. It's all evil!" the Buddhist said through cracked and scalded lips, staring mesmerized into the white-hot conflagration inside the room. The moisture on his retinas was boiling and sizzling as he continued to peer into the light. Bryant shielded his eyes and stepped into the room.

It took a moment before he could see anything at all. Then his eyes located Farrington who was standing up shouting jubilantly as semen erupted from his rigid penis in a copious spray. His ejaculate bathed the enraptured visage of a gelatinous misshapen blob of a woman who sat beneath him with her face turned up toward his and her tongue outstretched to receive his seed like some twisted communion. Farrington's eyes were fixed on another woman across the room from which the light seemed to be emanating. Her body looked like someone had wrung it out like a dishrag. Her limbs curled and twisted like crazy straws. But she was giving birth to something, something too big for her vaginal passage that was tearing her apart in its haste to be born. The being seemed to be composed of pure light.

"God! God has come!"

Bryant heard Farrington shout excitedly.

"That—that can't be God. No fucking way God would split someone apart like that." Bryant thought as the entity tore its way out of poor Sharon, cauterizing the huge avulsion it ripped in her torso as it shrugged out of her flesh like a diver crawling out of a wet-suit, turning her twisted body inside out. The light was so brilliant that Bryant could feel it burning his skin.

Bryant was struck dumb by the scene. He didn't know what he'd expected to find when he busted into the room but it was definitely not this. He stood rooted to the spot with the Beretta pointed uselessly at the floor. The blazing phosphorescence seemed to be consuming the entire room. The walls, ceilings, floor, the entire mansion disappeared like a desert mirage leaving only the light, as spectacular as an exploding star. It was as if the sun itself had come down from the heavens and into the room with them. Bryant continued to stare. His mind unraveling as logic failed him, unable to reason away what was so clearly beyond reason.

(XVII)

Farrington stumbled forward, knocking the fat limbless woman aside as he approached the light and fell to his knees in awe. This was it. This was what he'd been working so hard for all these years. Finally, God had come. His head filled with a universe of colors as starlight washed over him and into him.

"It's so beautiful! My God! Finally! You have come!"

The billionaire trembled with delight as he narrowed his eyes against the searing glare, trying to glimpse the entity within.

"I AM ALL! I AM EVERYTHING! I AM THE TRUTH!" The voice shook the room and seemed to vibrate through every molecule.

"Show yourself! Let me see you!" Farrington shrieked as his tear ducts emptied and the tears sizzled down his cheeks.

Gradually, the startling pyrotechnics died down. Farrington squinted through the diminishing light and his mouth widened in a perfect O as the scream ripped its way up from his diaphragm and the shadow within the light revealed itself.

The entity materializing before him could not have been God. Nothing in or in sight of heaven could have been so profane and hideous. The monstrous thing was a chaos of limbs and mouths, genitals of every sex and species, and suppurating orifices with purposes that seemed beyond appetite or reproduction. Tentacles stretched out in all directions from its bloated body feeding down into the earth and off into the distance. Farrington's eyes followed one fat slimy appendage, which lead from the hideous thing directly into the top of his own skull.

"W-what are you?" Farrington whispered, utterly appalled at the abomination he'd invoked. He could now feel the creature's tentacle crawling around between his thoughts. It's presence felt more familiar than alien. He felt no pain as if it had not been suddenly thrust there but had always been there and only just now revealed.

"I AM LUST. I AM AVARICE. I AM GREED. I AM LEVIATHAN!"

Its voice was a chorus of roars and hisses, howls, moans, and screams. Every sound that had haunted man's nightmares since he shivered in dark caves still only dreaming of fire. The light was now completely gone and in its place was a dank humid fog that seemed to coat everything with a sweaty film as if the creature was emanating some foul noxiousness.

"YOU CALLED ME AND I HAVE COME."

"But...but I didn't call you! I called for GOD!" Farrington shrieked, delirious with fear.

"GOD? BUT I AM GOD. I AM THE GOD OF MAN. NOT THE CREATOR BUT THE INNOVATOR. ALL THAT MAN HAS WROUGHT HAS BEEN WITH MY INSPIRATION. I AM EVIL AND MANKIND IS MY INSTRUMENT."

An endless sea of mouths smiled out at Farrington from the creature's enormous bulk and tongues slithered out to lick the thing's vulgar lips. Farrington felt the tentacle move inside his head as the thing leaned in close.

"LET ME SHOW YOU WHAT I AM."

And Farrington saw...

Teenagers mugging old ladies to buy drugs. Kids even younger murdering other adolescents over gang turf. Prostitutes swapping diseases with sex-addicts in dank alleys and semen-stained motel sheets. Rapists plundering and bruising the loins of screaming victims. Sexual predators using surrogate penises of sharpened steel to open the tender flesh of their dying lovers. Pedophiles abusing children. Terrorists bombing embassies. Satanists sacrificing babies. Murderers, cannibals, thieves, wife-beaters, drug-dealers, every manner of evil in the world, all with this demon's tentacles manipulating it, orchestrating the madness. Perhaps God valued freewill, if there truly was such a thing, but to this creature man was little more than a marionette, a toy for its perverse amusements.

Farrington was impressed. This was not God but it was something much better. This was a different type of perfection. Perfect evil. Something the billionaire understood and even more, could emulate. He didn't have tentacles with which to fiddle with the minds of humanity but he had other resources, money, computers, an entire global network. His control could easily surpass that of the creature who stood before him now. But it wouldn't help him to turn the angels. For that he needed more power. He needed the ability to control minds and wills as this creature obviously could.

"Show me how," he said.

(XVIII)

Westmore had no idea what he was walking into. He'd been just a few doors down releasing the religious leaders from captivity, at least the ones not already enthralled by the Metopronil, when he'd seen the light explode down the hallway and heard that voice like the shrieks of the damned. He knew right away that Farrington had unleashed something and it damned sure wasn't God. He unlocked the last door and turned to race toward the cacophony when he was nearly trampled by two seven-foot albinos.

The platinum-skinned giants tore past him and charged into the room where the light had already extinguished itself. Westmore recognized them from Bryant's description. The angels. He gripped the axe in his hand and ran after them, afraid of what would happen to Bryant if he were in that room alone with the owner of that horrible voice and those two colossal twins.

The photographer had only taken a few steps when the angel appeared before him again looking even more scruffy and unkempt than before. His five o'clock shadow was now becoming a full beard. The Bob Dylan look-a-like cast him a look that could only be described as panic. It was terrible to see on a being that was immortal. If he was afraid than Westmore should have been terrified.

"Hurry!" the angel shouted.

A flood of horrible images flooded through his mind the force of them staggering him and nearly knocking him to the floor. He saw a world where rape, murder, and torture were canonized and innocence and love was just a memory. It was the world that Farrington would bring about. Westmore steeled his resolve and ran past the charred body of a naked Asian man and into the room. As he ran past him, the little Asian man's eyes opened and stared right into his.

"Hurry!" the monk croaked out in a hoarse ragged bark and then he shuddered and his eyes closed again. Westmore was sure the man had died. He stepped inside what remained of the room just as Farrington seemed to be intercoursing with a demon that looked like some type of anemone that had floated up from the bottom of the sea. Bryant was standing a few feet away with a gun in his hands pointed at the demon and a look on his face that suggested his consciousness had fled his body. Westmore grabbed him and shook him.

"James! James wake up! You have to shoot Farrington! You have to kill him!"

The angels had launched themselves at the demon and were tearing into it with their long spiraled nails. Their nails snapping even as they rent through the thing's flesh. They sank their teeth into it and began ripping chunks out of it. The creature howled in pain. Then Westmore saw what they were trying to do. They were trying to sever the tentacle that led from the creature into Farrington's head. Westmore charged with the axe and began hacking away at it as well.

"James! James! Wake up!"

A thick black goop sprayed out of the creature with every swing of the axe and it fought back, filling his head with the most vile and horrible images. His stomach rolled and he pitched forward and projectile vomited in a spray that flew almost into the hallway. But he continued to swing the axe.

"I see! I see!" Farrington shrieked as the demon filled his head with the knowledge of perfect evil. The fat limbless woman who had been sucking down his seed was now cringing away from him trying to back her way out the door. Farrington grabbed her by the hair and pulled her back over to him. He dug his fingers into her skull and it began to crack. Blood poured from her nose, ears, mouth, and even her eyes as he ripped her head in half and dashed her gray-matter onto the floor at his feet. Then the angels attacked him.

Giving up on cutting through the demon's coarse limb, they tackled Farrington and began trying to sever the man's head from his neck and shoulders using only their teeth.

Westmore jumped down and raised the axe above his head ready to cleave the billionaire's head in two when gunshots rang out and the man's chest exploded. Westmore looked up and saw his partner standing above him pointing the gun down at Farrington and pumping bullet after bullet into his torso.

"I saw it. I saw what he was trying to become. I don't know how but I could see it all." Bryant hovered above the dead billionaire still aiming the 9mm down at him as if expecting him to get up again. "It was so horrible, man. You don't know what he would have become. I had to kill him. I couldn't let him…it was just so terrible, so evil."

"I know, man. We all saw it. It's okay. You had to kill him."

Bryant suddenly remembered the demon and turned to empty the rest of his clip into the hideous thing but it was already crawling away as smoke and flames ate their way through the floorboards and began to consume the house.

"Shit! I almost forgot about the fire! This whole place is about to go up!" Westmore shouted as he ran for the door where smoke had already filled the hallway. A wall of fire was inching its way down the hall cutting off their retreat.

"Oh shit we're trapped! Watch out!"

Farrington wasn't dead yet. His body was changing, breaking down and reforming, morphing into something that resembled the demon they had just chased away. A nest of tentacles wormed their way out of his ruptured chest and stomach reaching out for Bryant and the two twins. The twins bared their teeth like wild animals snarling in fury. Bryant turned and fired. One bullet slammed into Farrington's throat, tearing out his larynx and lodging in his vertebrae, then the gun dry-fired on an empty chamber. Farrington smiled. He picked the young journalist up with one of his serpentine appendages and tossed him out into the hall, into the fire.

"Nooooo!"

Bryant's body sailed past and Westmore rushed to rescue him. He pulled Bryant free of the flames just as the man began to scream.

"He's still alive! He's still alive!" Bryant was in a near panic.

"Nothing we can do about that now. We've got to get out of here. The entire mansion is burning down!"

They looked back into the room and saw Farrington rise up and spread his arms wide to embrace the twins. Tentacles exploded from every surface that would permit them, growing longer and thicker. He smiled as the angels rushed into his arms and then began to cry out as they sank their teeth into him. The three of them fell to the ground struggling, trying to kill each other. Westmore grabbed Bryant and they both sprinted down the hallway away from the flames.

"There's a pool down at the end of the hall. It has windows in there that we can break. We can get out that way."

Behind them they could hear the billionaire screaming for his life as the angels tore into him and the fire spilled into the room. The fire continued down the hall, licking at their heels and roaring in their ears as it sucked the oxygen out of the air and scorched their lungs. They ripped open the door to the poolroom and fell through it just as the flames had begun to blister the skin on their backs.

There was no time to try to break out one of those Lexan windows. There were no more bullets in the gun and nothing else in the poolroom would have been strong enough to shatter them. Bryant and Westmore dove into the pool as the poolroom door exploded and a burst of super-heated air came blasting in.

They could still hear Farrington's screams as they sank beneath the chlorinated water. The angels were tearing him apart and what they didn't destroy the fire certainly would. Nothing could have survived that inferno.

(XIX)

The water was getting warmer. There were no flammable surfaces within the poolroom, which was covered from floor to ceiling in 17" Gialo Antiqua marble tiles imported from Italy preventing the fire from spreading right to the pool's edge, but the rest of the estate was burning down and the water temperature was quickly reaching the boiling point.

The windows exploded from the heat. The two journalists leapt up out of the pool and ran for daylight as fast as they could. Their skin blistered as the intense heat seared their flesh. Their eyes watered, obscuring their vision. They closed their eyelids and dove headfirst through the shattered windows.

Westmore crashed through a row of shrubbery and rolled out into the big circular driveway where the limo that had brought them to this madhouse still sat. He looked around him for Bryant but the man was nowhere to be found. Then he looked back up at the window he'd just leapt through and saw Bryant still crouched on the window ledge...wrapped in tentacles. He saw the reporter's eyes bulge out of their sockets and his brains squirt out of his ears when the tentacles constricted and his bones snapped and collapsed, his body being slowly crushed.

"James! Noooo!" Westmore cried out as Bryant was dragged back into the flames. Moments later the entire mansion collapsed.

(XX)

It had been more than a year since Westmore had been back to the site where the Farrington mansion once stood. In that time he'd been besieged with requests for interviews about the murderous zealot and exorbitant offers for the purchase of his pictures of the mansion and its activities. He'd refused them all. He couldn't bring himself to profit in anyway from what had taken place here. And more than that, he didn't want that madman's story told. That's why he had brought them there in the first place, to tell his story, that's why Bryant had died. He didn't want to give that lunatic the satisfaction. He would take the tale to his grave instead. Still, there was one last photograph he wanted to get. It would be the only one he'd ever publish involving this place.

Richard Westmore crept tentatively through the rubble and ash that was all that remained of Farrington's estate. He made his way to the place where the freaks had been kept, where indescribable atrocities had transpired and there, just where the angel had told him it would be, bloomed a white lotus. Westmore looked up at the sky as the sun peeked through the clouds. He smiled and wiped the tear from his eye then he knelt and snapped a picture.

HOW TO BECOME A TERATOLOGIST: AN INTERVIEW WITH EDWARD LEE AND WRATH JAMES WHITE
BY DAVE HINCHBERGER

ter·a·tol·o·gist. A specialist in teratology. The science or study of monstrosities or abnormal formations in organisms. –*Dictionary.com Unabridged (v 1.1)*

Teratologist is the first collaboration between Edward Lee and Wrath James White. This novel had a short print run from a previous publisher and is now re-released in a special signed limited edition from Overlook Connection Press. This edition features original cover art by Alan Clark and is completely re-typeset in this new release.

Teratologist introduced many readers to author Wrath James White for the first time. Edward Lee has also co-authored works of horror with authors Jack Ketchum and John Pelan. For this *Teratologist* release from the Overlook Connection Press, publisher Dave Hinchberger has brought these two authors together to discuss their collaboration on this novel.

《《—》》

DAVE: First, let's discover the origins of your collaboration together: Lee, you've co-authored several works with John Pelan, Jack Ketchum, and others. How does this work? How did Lee and White come together to work on this project?

LEE: Actually I've collaborated with a number of authors on various projects, including some guy named Ketchum. As for The *Teratologist*, it was strangely coincidental as I recall; about that time, I'd begun reading some of Wrath's short fiction–and really digging it–when John Turi asked me if I'd be interested in collaborating on a short story with Wrath. I was in between deadlines right then, so I said hell yeah. I'd met Wrath only once previously, at one of the Horrorfind cons. Anyway, the idea of collaborating with this extreme-fiction juggernaut sounded like it would be a ton of fun. I had a very basic concept floating around in my head, so I ran it by Wrath and he liked it, but it was still very basic. We thought we'd see how it went, so I wrote the first chunk and realized that the "basic" concept I'd contributed wasn't good enough to produce anything more than just a gross-out piece; thankfully, though, Wrath came up with a fantastic accentuation of that basic concept which wound up giving the piece a lot of brains and outrageous spirituality. So that's when this "short story" jumped out of the gate and became a pretty unique novella.

WHITE: As I recall Lee and I were both at a Horror convention. I believe it was World Horror in Chicago. Brian Keene brought me over and introduced me to Lee who, coincidentally, was one of the writers everyone had been telling me I had to read because our styles were so similar. I had just started reading his work a week or two before the convention. At that time I really didn't read a lot of horror even though that was about all I wrote. I was more into psychological thrillers, philosophy, and S&M erotica at that time. An up and coming publisher caught the exchange between the two of us and suggested that we do a collaboration. An opportunity like that was an absolute dream come true for me so I quickly agreed. I had no idea the impact it would have on my career. I owe the man a lot.

DAVE: Reading the novel, I thought content flowed fairly well considering two writers came together to bring us one storyline. One of you must have had the idea for TERATOLGIST first. Who started the novel and how did you share responsibilities to make it work?

LEE: See above. The basic concept–I keep calling it–occurred to me in a moment of creative revulsion when I bought a book printing in the 1930's (I think) called MEDICAL CURIOSITIES. It was a legitimate reference book for doctors which detailed known congenital defects in humans, and it was harrowingly grotesque. It didn't even have photographs as I recall, just drawings, and to this day I can't look at it anymore. Anyway, the fucked-up writer in me wondered: "What about a story about a guy who kidnaps the most heinously deformed victims for sexual purposes?" That was my initial contribution which, on its own, was pretty thin and definitely one of those gross-for-the-sake-of-gross deals. Then Wrath says: "but what if its a malefactor kidnapping these unfortunates for a distinct purpose: to commit crimes so foul and offensive–such as forcing priests, nuns, monks, etc. to have sex with the victims–that the crimes would challenge God to appear?" That's when it took off. And it was fun: I'd write a chunk, then Wrath would write the next chunk, then me, and then him, like that, and because the two protagonists bare suspicious similarities to Wrath and me, we would find each other swapping roles. I'd be writing the Wrath character and he'd be writing the Lee character. It was a hoot. As for the actual word-count in the end, Wrath wrote about 60 percent and I wrote 40. It's the only time I've done a collaboration in sequence like that–a lot of times they don't work–but this worked so well I was sorry when the story was completed.

WHITE: I remember *Teratologist* being primarily Lee's idea. After we agreed to collaborate, Lee emailed me with the idea to do a story about an eccentric billionaire who collected human oddities and forced them into sexual congress with religious leaders. At least I think the religious leader thing was his idea. Time has made some of the details a little fuzzy. I thought it would be interesting to give him a more grandiose motive then simple perversion and came up with the idea to have him perform these heinous sacrilegious acts in order to enrage God enough to where he would be forced to reveal himself allowing the antagonist an opportunity to attempt to steal his power. Lee agreed and the rest is history.

We decided to write the story in two thousand word blocks until the project was finished. Sometimes we wrote more or less depending on our level of inspiration and available time. I don't want to give away the order in which we wrote the stories. Half the fun of it is trying to figure out who wrote what. So far everyone who has tried has gotten it wrong, including a good friend of ours who has proofread both of our work on numerous occasions. I think our styles blended amazingly well.

DAVE: The idea of having God, or a deity, to be forced to come forth and face evil created by this man on Earth, was an interesting one indeed. This was the first time I'd read author White. However as an avid reader of Lee's work, I found this to be, at least graphically so, along the lines of Lee's THE BIGHEAD. Was the idea to be so graphic always part of the idea?

WHITE: From the basic concept of a man obsessed with human deformities, even before I put my blasphemous spin on it, it was destined to be extremely graphic. With our two styles of writing, which are both rather intense, there was no way the book could have turned out any other way, especially not with such a great set up. Religious leaders, human oddities, and sex, how else could it have turned out?

DAVE: Understood (laughs). This next question you may not want to answer, but I'm asking anyway: were any of the characters in *Teratologist* based on any "real" characters in your own lives or the world in general?

WHITE: For me, besides the two main characters of course, it was all "off the dome". I just imagined the deformities and then imagined what I would be like if I possessed that particular defect, what my life and personality would be like, then I exaggerated the hell out of it. Most of my characters do tend to be sort of an amalgamation of various character traits I've observed in people over the years. I am a compulsive people watcher so I couldn't even tell you who I picked up what from. I watch everyone. I'm that creepy dude in the corner that makes you feel uncomfortable when you catch him staring at you. But if you're asking if I ever dated anyone liked the Twins or picked up someone like Betty or Sharon for a one night stand, the answer is not that I can recall.

LEE: That was part of the challenge, fictionalizing these tragic deformities, most of which, though rare, do exist, and then trying to integrate characters in the mix—FUCKED UP characters but characters nonetheless. But don't worry, I swear I didn't slip in any secret sexual fantasies of my own. Not in this book at any rate...

DAVE: Wrath, you mentioned that during the time you met Lee you had not read that much horror even though you were writing it. Since the first publication of *Teratologist* have you had an opportunity to read some of the writers in the horror field today? If yes, has this had any effect on your current writing?

WHITE: My recent writings are a lot less sexual than when I first began. My first attempts at writing horror were sort of accidental. I originally wanted to write erotica/pornography. I submitted a few erotica stories that I thought I'd spice up by adding elements of horror to them and the rejections came back indicating that perhaps I should try submitting them to horror publishers so I chopped out a bunch of the sex scenes and started submitting, having not read horror in more than a decade. The response was pretty amazing. Everyone thought what I was doing was so over the top, and it was, but that was mostly due to my ignorance of the genre. I just assumed that since movies, television, music, pornography, and even sports had gone more extreme than horror had surely followed suit if not led the movement. I had also just finished reading Poppy Z. Brite's Exquisite Corpse, which I still credit with rekindling my interest in horror. I was not trying to be controversial or extreme at all. I was trying to fit in and write the type of things I enjoyed, wrongly assuming that all horror had progressed to the type of boundary-free taboo-free writing I enjoyed. I was expecting everything to look like Exquisite Corpse. I wasn't even aware that there was such a thing as extreme horror. I was just writing the kind of stuff I would have wanted to read. And once I did start reading horror regularly I was going solely off recommendations, and based on what people had read of my work to that point, everyone recommended that I read Ed Lee.

Now, having read lots of Lee, and Ketchum, and Laymon, and Ray Garton, and Charlee Jacob, and Brian Keene as well as some of the more traditional authors, when I'm pushing the envelope, I'm at least aware of it. Not shocking the hell out of people unwittingly the way I used to. I'm also aware of what makes me different and so I don't tread as much on ground that has already been crossed as I have in the past. I have more awareness of my own strengths and weaknesses. I know that there are some authors that do certain things better than I could ever hope to, so I tend to stick to what I do best. Which isn't to say I don't take risks or try new things, you're just not likely to see a paranormal romance or a science fiction or dark fantasy novel out of me anytime soon. I may try my hand at more historical horror or horror based on hard science, because I have discovered that I really enjoy research. Still, psychological/philosophical/spiritual and religious horror seems to be my niche.

DAVE: Lee, you have quite a loyal following, I would almost say cult-like. My experience with your readers is once they read you, they clamor for more and anxiously await your next work. The lines at the horror cons to meet you are ever-growing. How has *Teratologist* been received by your readers? Have you ever had readers ask for sequels to any co-authored works?

LEE: The response I got from *Teratologist* was all very positive, which is proof that Wrath and I met the expectations of the readership. Loyal readers–God bless them–do frequently have favorites they'd like to see sequelized, and several have asked about this as well as other collaborations I've done. The problem with sequels–even though I do a lot of them–is you really have to have an idea that takes the original plot in another direction. (It you don't, it's no fun to write, and sure as hell wouldn't be any fun to read!) Wrath and I pretty much popped the aesthetic gourd on *Teratologist*, so there'd be no point in carrying it on. One of these days, though, we probably will collaborate on another story but it would have to be totally different, a complete new vision. Hmm. Paranormal romance, maybe. Just kidding!

DAVE: Wrath, what has been your experience with readers concerning *Teratologist*? If someone is reading you for the first time with *Teratologist* what would you recommend they read by you next now that they've got their feet wet so-to-speak?

WHITE: I have not met anyone, whether they're fans of extreme horror or not, who does not love this book. As Lee said earlier, it is so much more than just a gross-out horror novella. It has a lot of spiritual and philosophical aspects to it. One reader referred to it as "extreme religious horror." If someone really liked *Teratologist* then I'd definitely recommend they read Poisoning Eros co-authored with Monica O'Rourke and my collection The Book of A Thousand Sins. Both have the same religious and philosophical underpinnings that *Teratologist* has although The Book of A Thousand Sins is probably a little more heavy-handed in that regard. But there's enough sex and violence and pure gross-out that the reader shouldn't feel like they're being preached to.

DAVE: I realize that you both have individual writer careers but since you mentioned that writing *Teratologist* was such a rewarding experience do you think there's a possibility of another Lee / White story in the future?

WHITE: I would love to. I'm not ashamed to admit that I'm still a fawning fan when it comes to Lee's work. While I was writing *Teratologist* I think I tried to buy everything Lee had ever published. I recently ran right out and bought Slither the minute it hit the stands. Great book by the way, Lee. Creeped the hell out of me. I can't wait to pick up House Infernal. So... anyway... yeah, I'd love to.

LEE: See above. (Additionally, I was floored by Poisoning Eros. Highly recommended work.) Wrath and I have talked briefly about co writing something again down the road. He's really a ton of fun to write with as well as a creative workhorse. I'm sure that some day when we both have time, we'll come up with something that will kick out the jams of grotesquery in fiction. I almost shudder to think what it might be...

«« — »»

More titles by Edward Lee and Wrath James White.

EDWARD LEE:

The Backwoods, The Bighead, The Chosen, City Infernal, Coven, Creekers, Flesh Gothic, Gast, Ghouls, Goon (co-authored with John Pelan), *House Infernal, Incubi, Infernal Angel, Messenger, Monstrosity, Sacrifice, Succubi.* Upcoming: *The Order of the Scarlet Nuns* (tentative title—Edward Lee's first "vampire" novel,) *Golemesque,* and *Minotauress* (a prequel, of sorts, to Edward Lee's novella *The Horn-Cranker*).

WRATH JAMES WHITE:

The Book of A Thousand Sins His Pain, Broken (twisted gore-soaked tales of sex death and pain), co-authored with Alex Severin and Hertzan Chimera, *Hero* co-authored with J.F. Gonzalez (2007 release), *Poisoning Eros* co-authored with Monica O'Rourke, *Succulent Prey, Teratologist* co-authored with Edward Lee.

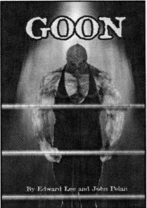

GOON

by Edward Lee & John Pelan

- Author's Preferred Version
- Original cover art by Erik Wilson
- Seven Original/Graphic Interior Illustrations by Micah Hayes.
- Signed Limited Edition Hardcover 1/500 red titles
  $44.95
- HARD COVER: ISBN 1-892950-62-6—yellow titles
  $39.95
- 1/26 Lettered FULL GRAIN Leather edition in wood box. SIGNED by both Authors **$275.00**

Six-foot-nine and four hundred pounds, hailing from parts unknown, he is the one-man walking gore-machine of the Deep South Wrestling Conference, and his name is...

GOON

But police captain Philip Straker isn't a wrestling fan. The bodies pile up like dirty laundry: sex-obsessed tramps used as playthings by some unspeakable creature. Is it just a coincidence, or do all the victims have something in common?

GOON

Investigative reporter Melinda Pierce will do anything to find out, by offering herself up as a sexual spittoon in order to infiltrate the lust-drenched warrens of backstage wrestling. She partakes in carnal forays so gross, so downright nasty, they'd make Linda Lovelace bend over and puke. All to track down...

GOON

Is Goon just a wrestler gone insane? Or is he something hideously worse? Relentless as a Texas Deathmatch, GOON is a no-holds-barred festival of body slams and insatiable orgy, of piledrivers and sexual grotesquerie, of neckbreakers, drop-kicks and more blood and guts than a fish market floor. It just might leave you down for the count...

The notorious long-sold-out classic of modern horror is back! The Overlook Connection is proud to present this newly illustrated and one of the most talked about—and outrageous—tales to ever be penned in the horror genre.

"A raunchy riot of rasslin', ringrats, and no-holds-barred sex. A must for fans of over-the-top action and outrageous thrills."
—Lucy Taylor, author of *The Safety of Unknown Cities* and *The Silence Between The Screams*

 OVERLOOK CONNECTION PRESS
PO Box 1934 • Hiram, GA • 30141
PHONE: 678-567-9777 • FAX: 770-222-6192
EMAIL: overlookcn@aol.com
www.overlookconnection.com

THE BIGHEAD IS COMING...HE'S COMING...FOR YOU!

The Bighead
by Edward Lee

- Trade Paperback   ISBN: 1-892950-13-8 $24.95
- Hard Cover-Signed   ISBN: 1-892950-41-3 $44.95

AUTHOR'S
PREFERRED VERSION
ORIGINAL COVER ART &
INTERIORS BY ERIK WILSON

"Edward Lee is to horror novels what Spain and S. Clay Wilson were to Underground Comics over twenty-five years ago— funny, evil, perverse as it is humanly possible to get...and gleefully outrageous about it. I'd say we got us a whole new sub-genre goin' here, boys and girls—splatterspunk!"
—JACK KETCHUM, author of *Off Season*, and *The Girl Next Door*

RAPE. MURDER. BRAIN-EATING...

THE BIGHEAD
Who is he? What is he? An inbred homicidal pervert? A supernatural psychopath? Who or whatever he is, he's on a roll now, raging out of the Virginia backwoods, and leaving in his wake a trail of blood, guts, and disgust far beyond the limits of your reckoning.

JERRICA
Sex-addict, drug-addict—a woman so far out of control she would make Linda Lovelace look like a schoolmarm. And little does she know, The Bighead is coming...for her.

THE ABBEY
Closed for years, Wroxeter Abbey is back in business, haunted by two nuns...from hell. Erotopathic, clinically demented, gross beyond belief. To the faithful priest, Father Alexander, they will do things that absolutely beggar description...

Never before has a work of fiction dared to delve so deeply into the realms of perversion, sexual dementia, and bad taste.

OVERLOOK CONNECTION PRESS
PO Box 1934 • Hiram, GA • 30141
PHONE: 678-567-9777 • FAX: 770-222-6192
EMAIL: overlookcn@aol.com
www.overlookconnection.com

Printed in the United Kingdom by
Lightning Source UK Ltd., Milton Keynes
141369UK00002B/16/A

9 781892 950857